UNDER THE DIEHARD BRAND

SELECTED FICTION WORKS BY
L. RON HUBBARD

FANTASY
The Case of the Friendly Corpse

Death's Deputy

Fear

The Ghoul

The Indigestible Triton

Slaves of Sleep & The Masters of Sleep

Typewriter in the Sky

The Ultimate Adventure

SCIENCE FICTION
Battlefield Earth

The Conquest of Space

The End Is Not Yet

Final Blackout

The Kilkenny Cats

The Kingslayer

The Mission Earth Dekalogy*

Ole Doc Methuselah

To the Stars

ADVENTURE
The Hell Job series

WESTERN
Buckskin Brigades

Empty Saddles

Guns of Mark Jardine

Hot Lead Payoff

A full list of L. Ron Hubbard's
novellas and short stories is provided at the back.

*Dekalogy—a group of ten volumes

L. RON HUBBARD

UNDER THE DIEHARD BRAND

GALAXY PRESS

Published by
Galaxy Press, LLC
7051 Hollywood Boulevard, Suite 200
Hollywood, CA 90028

Printed in the United States of America.

ISBN-10 1-59212-261-2
ISBN-13 978-1-59212-261-5

Library of Congress Control Number: 2007927537

CONTENTS

STORIES FROM PULP FICTION'S GOLDEN AGE

A ND it *was* a golden age.

The 1930s and 1940s were a vibrant, seminal time for a gigantic audience of eager readers, probably the largest per capita audience of readers in American history. The magazine racks were chock-full of publications with ragged trims, garish cover art, cheap brown pulp paper, low cover prices—and the most excitement you could hold in your hands.

"Pulp" magazines, named for their rough-cut, pulpwood paper, were a vehicle for more amazing tales than Scheherazade could have told in a million and one nights. Set apart from higher-class "slick" magazines, printed on fancy glossy paper with quality artwork and superior production values, the pulps were for the "rest of us," adventure story after adventure story for people who liked to *read*. Pulp fiction authors were no-holds-barred entertainers—real storytellers. They were more interested in a thrilling plot twist, a horrific villain or a white-knuckle adventure than they were in lavish prose or convoluted metaphors.

The sheer volume of tales released during this wondrous golden age remains unmatched in any other period of literary history—hundreds of thousands of published stories in over nine hundred different magazines. Some titles lasted only an issue or two; many magazines succumbed to paper shortages during World War II, while others endured for decades yet. Pulp fiction remains as a treasure trove of stories you can read, stories you can love, stories you can remember. The stories were driven by plot and character, with grand heroes, terrible villains, beautiful damsels (often in distress), diabolical plots, amazing places, breathless romances. The readers wanted to be taken beyond the mundane, to live adventures far removed from their ordinary lives—and the pulps rarely failed to deliver.

In that regard, pulp fiction stands in the tradition of all memorable literature. For as history has shown, good stories are much more than fancy prose. William Shakespeare, Charles Dickens, Jules Verne, Alexandre Dumas—many of the greatest literary figures wrote their fiction for the readers, not simply literary colleagues and academic admirers. And writers for pulp magazines were no exception. These publications reached an audience that dwarfed the circulations of today's short story magazines. Issues of the pulps were scooped up and read by over thirty million avid readers each month.

Because pulp fiction writers were often paid no more than a cent a word, they had to become prolific or starve. They also had to write aggressively. As Richard Kyle, publisher and editor of *Argosy*, the first and most long-lived of the pulps, so pointedly explained: "The pulp magazine writers, the best of them, worked for markets that did not write for critics or attempt to satisfy timid advertisers. Not having to answer to anyone other than their readers, they wrote about human beings on the edges of the unknown, in those new lands the future would explore. They wrote for what we would become, not for what we had already been."

Some of the more lasting names that graced the pulps include H. P. Lovecraft, Edgar Rice Burroughs, Robert E. Howard, Max Brand, Louis L'Amour, Elmore Leonard, Dashiell Hammett, Raymond Chandler, Erle Stanley Gardner, John D. MacDonald, Ray Bradbury, Isaac Asimov, Robert Heinlein—and, of course, L. Ron Hubbard.

In a word, he was among the most prolific and popular writers of the era. He was also the most enduring—hence this series—and certainly among the most legendary. It all began only months after he first tried his hand at fiction, with L. Ron Hubbard tales appearing in *Thrilling Adventures, Argosy, Five-Novels Monthly, Detective Fiction Weekly, Top-Notch, Texas Ranger, War Birds, Western Stories,* even *Romantic Range.* He could write on any subject, in any genre, from jungle explorers to deep-sea divers, from G-men and gangsters, cowboys and flying aces to mountain climbers, hard-boiled detectives and spies. But he really began to shine when he turned his talent to science fiction and fantasy of which he authored nearly fifty novels or novelettes to forever change the shape of those genres.

Following in the tradition of such famed authors as Herman Melville, Mark Twain, Jack London and Ernest Hemingway, Ron Hubbard actually lived adventures that his own characters would have admired—as an ethnologist among primitive tribes, as prospector and engineer in hostile climes, as a captain of vessels on four oceans. He even wrote a series of articles for *Argosy,* called "Hell Job," in which he lived and told of the most dangerous professions a man could put his hand to.

Finally, and just for good measure, he was also an accomplished photographer, artist, filmmaker, musician and educator. But he was first and foremost a *writer,* and that's the L. Ron Hubbard we come to know through the pages of this volume.

This library of Stories from the Golden Age presents the best of L. Ron Hubbard's fiction from the heyday of storytelling, the Golden Age of the pulp magazines. In these eighty volumes, readers are treated to a full banquet of 153 stories, a kaleidoscope of tales representing every imaginable genre: science fiction, fantasy, western, mystery, thriller, horror, even romance—action of all kinds and in all places.

Because the pulps themselves were printed on such inexpensive paper with high acid content, issues were not meant to endure. As the years go by, the original issues of every pulp from *Argosy* through *Zeppelin Stories* continue crumbling into brittle, brown dust. This library preserves the L. Ron Hubbard tales from that era, presented with a distinctive look that brings back the nostalgic flavor of those times.

L. Ron Hubbard's Stories from the Golden Age has something for every taste, every reader. These tales will return you to a time when fiction was good clean entertainment and the most fun a kid could have on a rainy afternoon or the best thing an adult could enjoy after a long day at work.

Pick up a volume, and remember what reading is supposed to be all about. Remember curling up with a *great story*.

—Kevin J. Anderson

KEVIN J. ANDERSON *is the author of more than ninety critically acclaimed works of speculative fiction, including The Saga of Seven Suns, the continuation of the Dune Chronicles with Brian Herbert, and his* New York Times *bestselling novelization of L. Ron Hubbard's* Ai! Pedrito!

UNDER THE DIEHARD BRAND

CHAPTER ONE

T HE night rider was nervous. It was with considerable effort that he kept his voice easy and assured as he sang. Two thousand longhorns, bedded down on the strange range country of Montana, moved restively, still upset after the dangerous crossing of the Missouri that day.

Summer lightning flashed in bright brass sheets along the horizon, momentarily showing up the semicircle of rimrock which surrounded the bed ground. The mutter of thunder growled across the sky. Bunched-up clouds shot nervously across the face of the moon.

The weary young trail hand knew there would be trouble before morning.

> "Sit down little cyows
> And rest yo' tails,
> An' forgit all about them dusty trails.
> Now if you played faro
> Or had a rival to yo' gal
> Yo' worries would be . . ."

He stopped suddenly and looked questioningly at the ridge to the south. Sheet lightning silhouetted a rider up there.

The trail hand rode a short distance from his charges to wave the strange horseman off from the nervous herd. The rider was coming slowly down the slope, being very careful to ride easily and quietly.

The trail hand advanced. "Howdy, stranger. Step light. These bovines is nervous wrecks after our crossin' today." He studied the other but asked no questions. He saw that the horse was travel-worn and knew from the other's rig and clothes that he had come through from Texas—which is a long jump.

"Sure. But they been mighty sparin' of signposts and I don't savvy this country none. Where's Wolf River?"

The trail hand looked more closely and saw that the stranger was young, around eighteen, and from the looks of him hadn't eaten very regularly of late. "The wagon's over to your right, stranger. Better go over and git down. We're short-handed and might be able to help you along."

"Thanks, but I been comin' for such a hell of a while that I'm gettin' anxious to see the target. You know Wolf River?"

"Some."

"Know if I can find Diehard Thompson there?"

"Sure you can. Last I hear of him, he's sheriff."

"Gettin' along all right?" said the stranger.

"Gettin' along in age," replied the trail hand. "Was a time when strong men fainted at the mention of that name, but the old boy's agin' up pretty bad. One of these days, somebody is goin' to get nerve enough to find out if he's as bulletproof as he used to be. He's slippin'. There's plenty of citizens—"

"Wait a minute," said the stranger, "you're talkin' about my dad."

"Hell, no offense, I hope. I didn't know Diehard ever

stopped practicin' the draw long enough to have a kid." He stopped uncomfortably. "Cooky'll fix you up if you drop over. You'd be plumb welcome to drift north with us, Thompson."

The youngster shifted wearily in his saddle and the trail hand noted the absence of all weapons.

"Guess I'll be swingin' on if you'll wise me up."

"Sure. Keep the Pole Star on your left a little. Wolf River's about sixty miles and if you miss it you'll fall over the GN tracks."

"Much obliged. Be seein' you."

The kid started a wide circle around the herd, picking his way by the flare of lightning. He was very thoughtful and a frown wrinkled up his tired face.

He traveled until he reached the other side of the bed ground and then looked up to pick out the Pole Star. Clouds were scudding across it, yellow in the lightning, blue white in the moonlight, and the task was difficult.

He had just singled it out when, behind him, he heard the far-off crack of a shot, almost blotted out by the summer thunder. He turned in his saddle and looked back.

He could see the whole amphitheater from where he sat. The cattle had started up, looking about, beginning to walk nervously in small circles.

He knew one rider could not hold that herd now and he reined around, intending to go back and be of what help he could.

Another shot made a thin red line on the ridge across.

The kid saw the trail hand as lightning fanned across the horizon. The man was laying on his quirt, racing away from the evident ambush, toward the far-off chuck wagon, going for help. The puncher streaked up the slope toward the ridge not far from the kid. The roll of the mustang's hoofs came faintly above the growing rumble in the herd.

An instant later, half a dozen horsemen rose magically on the rim above the trail hand, as black and stiff as though they had been cut from cardboard.

A heavyset fellow on a chunky horse spurred down to meet the puncher. Orange flame spat. Lightning flared.

The puncher leaned backwards in his saddle, hands thrown up. He vanished and his horse plunged on.

An instant later the others on the ridge started down, firing into the air, shouting.

The herd was ready to go. With a roll which shook the earth, two thousand longhorns began to stampede.

The cracking shots were blotted out in the crash of horns against horns. The riders were swallowed up in the geysering black dust.

The kid dug spur toward the unseen chuck wagon, quirting his weary horse. But his message was not needed. The fire was kicked together and tired men were struggling up, grabbing saddles and rifles.

The kid reached the spot where the riders had appeared first. He halted, waiting for the crew to come up to him. The trail hand was somewhere below. The kid walked his horse slowly down the slope.

Cattle were pouring over the far rim, bawling in terror, a seething cloud of madness on its express journey to nowhere.

The kid stopped again. Below him one of the riders had

reined in and dismounted beside the dead trail hand. The rider turned the body over with his foot. The arms flopped outward.

Above the booming storm of the departing stampede, the kid heard a resonant, unearthly, sad voice say, "God rest your soul, my man."

It was all one vast, scrambled nightmare to the kid, as illusive as cigarette smoke. The man just below could not see the kid against the black rocks and the kid, recovering reason in time, knew that it would be madness to show himself, unarmed, to this pious murderer.

The crew came boiling over the ridge. The mysterious rider had vanished completely. Suddenly the kid realized his precarious position, himself unknown in a strange country.

Lightning spread a yellow glare across the heavens. The kid spurred into the cover of the darkness. He looked back once as the sheet lightning flared again.

The trail hand was spread out in the form of a cross, his teeth bared in a cold grin, sightless eyes staring at the chilly moon.

CHAPTER TWO

TWO days later, the kid sidled uncertainly down the boardwalk raised above the dust of Wolf River. It was morning and the prairie sun was as warming as a drug. The denizens of the tough Montana cow town were rising and stretching and grumbling along the street, wondering why they had thought they could hold that much on the night before.

The kid spotted a squat red stone building over which drooped the sign "Jail. Sheriff's Office." He took a notch in his belt, straightened his battered Stetson, wiped the toes of his scuffed boots on the calf of each leg and advanced somewhat in the manner of a man about to lunge off his horse to grab the horns of a streaking steer.

He heard hoofbeats behind him but he was much too preoccupied with his own presence to turn. The riders were coming slowly.

The door to the office framed Diehard Thompson. He stepped from the sill to the walk and deliberately hooked his thumbs into his cartridge belt to survey the town with squinted, faded eyes. He looked in the kid's direction but not at the kid. Diehard's eyes popped open and he freed his hands, letting them swing down to the level of his lasheddown holsters. He took a deep breath.

The kid thought he had already been recognized, forgetting for the moment that his father had not seen him since Diehard's departure from Texas fifteen years before. The kid stopped.

Diehard's voice was querulous and worried but there was a hint of steel in it. "I thought I told you to stay clear of Wolf River!"

The voice which sounded behind the kid from the street was very familiar. It was a pious, sad voice with all the ringing intonation which rightly belonged to the pulpit.

"Are you starting that again, brother?"

The kid backed up against the building and stared at the riders. There were six of them, and in the lead, Holy George Gates was sorrowfully sitting his horse. The man was like a raven in his black frock coat. His eyes were too black and too bright. His jaw was long.

"I started it weeks ago," said Diehard Thompson, "and what I start I finish. There's been a herd stampeded and a trail hand killed. Where was you when it happened?"

Holy George put both hands on his pommel and mournfully regarded Diehard. "It is most unseeming, brother, for you to accuse me without cause. You should know that we were delivering beef to Fort Belknap."

"Whose beef?" said Diehard acidly.

"Beef legally and ethically purchased," said Holy George. "You forget I hold both the Army and railroad beef contracts."

"No man can fill them and still keep honest at the price *you* bid," snapped Diehard.

The riders sat very quietly, staring at Diehard. They were

a range-toughened lot, dust-covered and unshaven. The one at Holy George's right, Anvil Borse, nudged Holy George.

"What ya playin' with 'im for?" Anvil's voice was as big and as hard as the man. "You got the pull to—"

Holy George shook his head. "The poor old fellow is suffering from delusions. Pay no attention, Anvil."

Diehard took a threatening step forward. "I'm sufferin' from what? If you're looking for a war, Gates, I'm the man that can give it to you. I ain't as old and slow as some people seem to think, and when I told you to keep that rag-tailed bunch of hellions out of Wolf River, I meant what I said."

"Be careful," said Holy George sadly. "You forget your rheumatism, brother."

Diehard was shaking with rage, speechless. But Holy George turned his mount and his back to the sheriff and rode with his men down the street to Long Henry's Place, where they dismounted and trooped in.

A flat-faced and large-paunched man in somber civilian dress had been watching from the front of the Great Northern Hotel. He came waddling through the dust toward the sheriff's office.

"Diehard," said Johnny Simmons severely, "you've got to quit picking on Holy George Gates."

Diehard, like an old buffalo cornered by ravenous wolves, spun to face this new angle of attack. "Pickin' on him! Why, Jesus Jumpin' Jupiter! You talk like he was still in triangular pants. That murderin' wolverine would gut his own mother if he thought she had a dime in the house."

"Now, now, now," said Johnny Simmons. "You forget that as long as he deals through Wolf River, he's bringing money into the town."

"What kind of money?" wailed Diehard. "He's spillin' so much blood to get it, it's a wonder the Missouri don't turn pink!"

"Now, Diehard, you're getting short on temper. Maybe your rheumatism is hurting you this morning."

"Damn my rheumatism! If you don't quit making me pull up short every time I try to get at the bottom of all these raids and killings, I'll go as loco as a strychnined wolf. You're just like the rest of these psalm-singin' businessmen around here. As long as you get your money, you don't care how many men was killed."

"You're going too far. You forget who you're talking to."

"Naw, the smell ain't likely to let me forget that."

"Look here," roared Simmons, "you're so old you're bein' held together with balin' wire. If you was any kind of a sheriff you'd get out and really solve these murders instead of pickin' on Holy George just because his boys get wild when they come to town."

Diehard's dust-colored mustache stuck straight out from rage.

"You can't even handle this town!" cried Simmons, shouting him down. "Maybe you was a great gunman once. That was *once*. Nobody has seen you draw for three years. Every frontier criminal is heading for Wolf River just because of what they hear about the place being easy on them. We're bogged down to the hubs with vagrants and loafers. We're being stolen blind by petty thieves. And you won't do a thing about it. Unless you get busy here and now and clean up the riffraff of this town, I'll make it certain that you turn in your star! And lay off Holy George Gates!"

Diehard's rage had reached its peak and the fury of it had burned him out. He slumped suddenly and Simmons, seeing the abrupt looseness of the shoulders, pressed on. "You can start in right away and, if you mean business, you'll have this town clean by night."

Simmons waddled back through the dust of Wolf River and disappeared into the musty depths of his brick bank.

The kid still leaned against the side of the jail, looking at Diehard with hurt surprise on his face. Diehard was getting old. He was showing the effects of a life hazed with gun smoke. His face and eyes and mustache had all faded into a nondescript hue, a monotone of weariness.

He had always been slight and now age had thinned him even more. He looked very far from the man the West had once known as the most deadly lawman west of the Mississippi since the death of Wild Bill Hickok.

But the kid had ridden all the way from Texas, and though he knew the moment was wrong, he stepped up the walk and confronted Diehard.

Diehard became aware of him and looked him up and down with little interest. The kid did not make a very prepossessing picture. He was dusty and caked with dried mud. His neckerchief was tattered at the end like an old flag. The earth on his face was almost as thick as a plaster mask.

"What the hell do *you* want?" said Diehard.

The kid had forgotten many things. Diehard would not be likely to recognize his own son whom he had last seen in a cradle. Diehard had been too deep in the living of his own life to keep any check on his people.

Diehard was not thinking of his own boy. He thought he was still in Texas, pampered by his mother's parents, heir to a spread the size of an eastern state.

The kid had had a speech all planned. He had carefully schooled himself to say, "Father, I couldn't stand it down in the Panhandle and I've been two years getting to you. . . ." The schooling was smothered by Diehard's brusque manner.

"Well! Don't stand there gaping!" cried the badgered Diehard. "This town is getting so damned filled up with punks I can't even get through the streets. On your way."

"But—"

"If you're goin' to stay around Wolf River, get a job. If you ain't got one by sundown, you'll have to keep driftin'!"

Diehard turned and went into the office, leaving the kid standing forlorn and alone on the splintery boardwalk.

CHAPTER THREE

IT took the kid a couple of hours to realize that Diehard Thompson had apparently forgotten that he had once christened a son Lee Beauregarde Thompson. It required another hour for the kid to understand that the invincible Diehard had progressed into unhappy old age with rheumatism stiffening his gun arm until he was afraid to draw and discover how slow that once-lightning arm had become.

Although he could not express it, even to himself, the kid felt that Diehard was putting up a brusque front to cover up a soul sick with weary realization that his day was done.

Disconsolately, Lee Beauregarde wandered dustily across the street and into false-fronted Long Henry's Place. He was not sure why he went there and he was certainly not looking for the trouble with which he unwittingly collided.

He shut out the sunlight when he closed the door and paused, gazing through the smoke-blurred, fly-filled interior at Holy George Gates who was piously trying his slim white fingers at an innocent game of faro. But gazing at Holy George was so much like watching a funeral that the kid grew depressed, more than ever.

He sidled up to the bar and stood staring at the dill pickle and aged cheese which Long Henry was carelessly wont to call his "free lunch." Even so, the meager display was tantalizing to a stomach grown a stranger to food and coupled with a pocket lined only with tobacco crumbs.

The place was curiously noiseless. Cards slapped, men talked, but sound waves made small impression on the smoky atmosphere. Only one voice could penetrate the blue fog.

The kid cast his uneasy glance down along the ring-spotted mahogany and looked wonderingly at Anvil Borse. The man was wearing a blaring yellow shirt much grimed with grease and his boots were purple and white. The wide-brimmed, low-crowned Stetson was light tan and the neckerchief was a wondrous green.

Anvil Borse had a black beard a week old and a pair of obscene eyes. The kid had never seen a man so compactly built for battle. And as Holy George's foreman, the Russian had been getting plenty of that.

The kid turned his attention back to Holy George at the faro table. Holy George was as emotionless as a coffin, win or lose. The waxy white of his features was marred only by a scar on his left cheek—a livid mark which had the appearance of a blotched brand.

Raised in the tough Panhandle and on the trail for two long years, the kid had seen many case-hardened characters, had embroiled his young self with many armor-plated fists. But he had never seen a brace of men more deadly or more contrasted than the Russian and Holy George.

Anvil split the smoke with a boisterous laugh. One of the riders had said something which caught the full blast of Anvil's contempt.

"Him?" cried Anvil, waving his whiskey glass in an unsteady

circle. "*Him?* Naw, he couldn't stand ten seconds with Holy George! Aw, I admits that Diehard Thompson was plenty fast a long time ago and he laid plenty of corpses under the bunch grass, but that was a long time ago. He's scared stiff somebody is going to force him into an even break. Sure he is. Has he done anything in the last three years? Naw! And is he going to do anything? *Naw!* Holy George is so fast with his hide-out that he could beat his mirror reflection to the draw. Diehard wouldn't stand a chance, see?"

"Still," said the tipsy rider, "he was good once. Don't forget that."

"Sure. Yaw! But he ain't no good now. He's got a yaller streak down his back so wide you could trail a herd down it. He's all drawed up inside like he ate persimmons that wasn't ripe, he's so yaller. I tell you—"

The kid did not know how it happened. One minute the room was blue with smoke and next it was painted red with the flame of his wrath. The kid had a hundred and eighty pounds of muscle to back up his right fist and he could use it on occasion.

As the last "yaller" sounded, the kid was two feet from Anvil's right. He grabbed Anvil's shoulder and whirled him half around. The kid swung with everything he had and connected explosively with Anvil's stubbly beard.

The sound was like cracking a two-by-four.

Anvil's whiskey glass sailed, unspilling, straight up. It turned over at the top and streaked down, raining redeye on Anvil's twitching form. Anvil sat up, blinking. He saw a tattered youngster looming above him, both fists clenched,

The kid swung with everything he had and connected explosively with Anvil's stubbly beard.

grimy face set in a grin so awful that it would have done credit to an ogre.

Anvil brought his fists down like single jacks on the floor and shot himself erect in a trail of sparks. The third brimstone curse was just departing on its scorching path up Anvil's throat when the kid struck a second time.

Anvil spun as he went down. He upset a bright brass spittoon which went bowling musically off on a voyage across the dusty floor.

The kid dived downward through the shocked silence, scooped Anvil's ivory-handled single-action Army into his fist and came up on the other side of the prostrate man. Anvil turned over with a soulful groan and found out how his six-gun appeared from the underside.

Suddenly the kid was very weak in the knees. He leaned up against the bar and the gun dangled from his nerveless fingers. But he maintained an air of nonchalance as though he made a practice of going around pole-axing bigger and tougher foremen. He knew he was in for it and the memory of the night and summer lightning was dancing vividly before his eyes. The trail hand's eyes had been so glassy and Holy George's voice had been so deep.

His mental machinery was screaming out high-tension thought. But he grinned and let the gun dangle, being quite powerless now to move it. The place was so dark they could not see the greenish white line around his mouth as the sickness of reaction became powerfully physical.

He stood there and grinned and watched Holy George Gates get up and walk carefully toward him.

19

In tones which would have done credit to a tomb, Holy George said, "What's the idea, brother?"

The kid was thinking and now the thought arrived. He had to get out of this. He steadied his voice. He had been very close to shouting that no man could call his father yellow and get away with it. But hard on the heels of that he remembered that he might have been seen that night on the prairie and if they knew he was the son of Diehard Thompson, murder would be the least of their thoughts.

Standing there with five riders ready to plug him and Holy George only waiting to hear his answer before the hide-out came out blazing, the kid increased his grin, made it a go-to-hell affair.

"I didn't think he was so tough," said the kid. "A guy like Holy George Gates needs a foreman that can take care of himself. I'm electing yours truly to the job and if anybody has got any complaints, speak up and smoke up because I ain't a man to argue."

Holy George knew courage when he saw it. He also thought he knew men. He supposed that he saw here a rider on the owl-hoot trail, a puncher who liked a fight better than a meal. The kid was young but the West was full of youngsters who had acquired swift gun habits at a very early age.

Holy George saw something else. Tough Anvil Borse was discredited with the men—and this crew needed a man who could hit harder and draw faster than any one of them. It was beneath Holy George's dignity to attend to the details of that job.

Carefully and sadly, Holy George said, "Where you from, kid?"

"I'm from Nowhere and I'm on my way to Noplace and I got a hankering to go fast while I'm on the trail."

"You are from Texas, brother."

"That's as close to Nowhere as a man can get. Stay down!" This last to Anvil who was feebly trying to sit up. The kid's spur roweled his chest and he sank back.

Holy George looked around at the faces of his men. He saw they were all staring at the kid with awed respect.

"Brother," said Holy George, "you have procured yourself a job of work. We ride at dusk. Keep your mouth shut and use my credit for your clothes and guns."

The kid saved his thanks. He walked toward the door and Anvil sat up, got to his knees and then stood up. There was a brooding storm gathering in his eyes but he was saving it for a better time and a better place.

The kid turned back and sent the six-gun scooting along the floor. It brought up against Anvil's foot and he reached down and juggled it in his palm, watching the kid's retreating back.

The kid got outside and walked quickly up the walk. He passed the Great Northern Hotel and almost collided with Diehard.

"You still around?" growled the old lawman.

"Yeah," said the kid. "Yeah, I'm still around. Holy George Gates just hired me as his foreman and I'm stayin' around!"

Diehard's faded blue glance was wide with surprise. It softened and he scrubbed at his cheek. "What the devil, kid? You don't mean that."

"Sure I mean it."

Diehard looked remorseful. "Look here, sonny, I didn't

21

mean that kind of a job. You don't get the idea. If you swing in with Gates they'll be givin' you a necktie party one of these days as soon as the truth comes out. Listen to me, son. Don't hit the outlaw trail at your age. You'll wind up decoratin' a cottonwood tree. Look, I was pretty rough a while ago, but I didn't mean it. I . . . I was kind of upset. Listen. If you'll swing wide of that outfit I'll . . . I'll get you a job as deputy."

"Sorry," said the kid, walking off. "I got the job *I* want."

Diehard stood in the hot afternoon sunlight and watched the kid disappear into the general store. Wearily, Diehard turned and limped back toward the jail.

Chapter Four

THE following week, Holy George's outfit came back to Wolf River eating the dust of a thousand bawling longhorns destined for the railroad gangs employed on the Continental Divide.

Working ceaselessly, the men harassed the heaving brown sea into the loading pens, mustangs dashing back and forth to close up the stragglers.

The kid looked very different than he had on his first arrival in the town. His hat was new and stiff and his boots were as bright as his silver spurs. His buckskin shirt and chinks were spotless. Riding straight up, he made a handsome picture.

An old brush splitter, intuitively reading his doom in the chutes, tried to make a break for it. Head down and eyes wild, he plunged back against the stream, thundered past the kid and headed for the town.

The kid's buckskin wheeled on his hind legs and snare-drummed in pursuit.

Reaching down as they overtook the ladino, the kid grabbed the animal's tail and heaved hard to the left. The longhorn went down appetite over tin cup, plowing up a fog of yellow dust. Dazed, he got up, shaking his horns, walking in a circle. The kid's rope popped against his rump and the outlaw made haste to return to the protection of the herd.

Riding after him, the kid saw Diehard.

The old man was limping down toward the din of the pens, shoulders hunched as though he was cold. He glanced up as the kid passed him but neither spoke.

The cattle were all in now and Holy George's sweaty riders were drawing back, glad to have their wet stock penned, anticipating a day and night in Long Henry's Place and the high society of the Bird Cage Opera—"Fifty Girls Fifty."

Sitting aloof and solemn, Holy George looked quietly on. The kid rode up beside him, on the side where Holy George wore his blotched brand.

Johnny Simmons rode up, his stomach dented by his pommel, respectfully saluting Holy George. "You got a thousand head there?"

"Exactly a thousand," said Holy George mournfully.

"They told me to pay you now. You can leave it in my bank if you like."

"I need a few dollars to pay off the boys," said Holy George.

"Come on over and have a drink and I'll get it for you."

"All right, brother."

The two started ahead and then stopped. Diehard Thompson was standing resolutely in their path, faded eyes surveying them.

"What's the matter with you?" demanded Simmons.

Diehard hitched at his gun belt. "It don't take a telescope to see blotched brands among those cattle. That steer that just went down the street was a Mill Iron if I ever saw one."

"Get out of the way, you old fool," wheezed Simmons impatiently.

"I ain't movin'," said Diehard.

"Brother," said Holy George, "I told you once before that your interference was not welcome. And to that I'll add that unless you can produce *one single proof,* you had better keep still. You are going on slanderous guesses and I am not at all pleased."

"I don't care," said Diehard, "whether you're pleased or not. I'm tellin' you for the last time that you can get out of Wolf River and this county and stay out. And if you ever show your face here again, it's goin' to mean gun smoke."

The kid, some distance away, tensely sat his buckskin. He detected a slow, cruel pleasure creeping into Holy George's ascetic face. The kid looked at his father. Diehard was not backing down. The kid realized what this was costing the old man. For one last time he was going to match his old reputation against a faster gun.

Holy George straightened up. His ugly mouth was drawn down at the corners and the scar on his face was purple. "You're asking for it, brother. Make it an even break."

For an instant Diehard hesitated. His arm was almost paralyzed by rheumatism. But he showed no fear. In earlier years, too many men had gone down before him.

Diehard made a pass at his holster. He was slow.

Holy George had not seemed to move. Before Diehard had touched walnut, Holy George's short gun was centered on the sheriff's chest. Only one missing button, marked by its loose threads on the frocked coat, showed the passage of Holy George's hand.

Diehard was abruptly motionless, staring upward at the

hide-out's muzzle, momentarily expecting the impact of the killing shot.

But Holy George was not as kind as that. He had shown Wolf River that the old man was through. That was worse than killing.

"Now turn around," said Holy George, "and amble up the street and let's not see any more of you while I'm in Wolf River."

But the old man was too stunned to move. He flexed his stiff fingers as though to prove that they were empty of a gun. He could not believe that this thing had happened to him—that now he would be the butt of Wolf River's contempt.

Simmons' high, wheezing voice cut through the silence. "Damn you, Diehard, you've gone too far and now see what you've done! Damn you, get out of my sight! As soon as Charley Osmond gets back from Great Falls we'll have a meeting that'll show you where *you* stand."

Anvil and the riders guffawed uproariously behind Holy George.

Diehard slumped, turning painfully. He shuffled up the street toward his office, head down.

The kid did all he could to retain his fury. The raucous laughter of Holy George's hands was hard for him to bear.

But the kid was no fool. He sat his buckskin quietly and watched his father out of sight.

CHAPTER FIVE

T HE night was sharp as a saber. All that day long Vs of honking geese had been fleeing southward and even now made momentary patterns across the rising full moon, which rose into the midnight sky.

Seven punchers and Holy George Gates raced along the rough wagon trail which led into the heart of the Circle C range, eight scudding storm clouds.

The kid rode on Holy George's right. His chin thong cut his jaw and the wind made his ears feel brittle. From time to time he glanced at the grisly silhouette beside him and then back at the onrushing black blur which was Anvil Borse.

Day by day, Anvil had grown more and more bold, increasingly surly to the kid. More than once the kid had seen Anvil's hand resting upon the butt of the ivory-handled single-action Army while the man's cloudy black glare studied for a target. But Anvil did not want an even break. He was waiting, the kid knew, for the red turmoil of a fight in darkness.

And they rode now toward just such a scene.

The Army needed beef and the contract belonged to Holy George. The Circle C had just received a trail herd from the south and Holy George had spent the day in his cabin studying out the geometry of brands until he had discovered how to change the road brand, Lazy T, into his own Cross G from which had come his nickname.

Trail herds were so numerous and Circle C stock was so vast that he knew he could evade detection if he held his wet stock for a month—long enough for the brand marks to heal.

They came to a fork in the road and Holy George reined suddenly, bunching them up.

"Which way?" said Holy George. "The right?"

"Naw," said Anvil. "I got 'em spotted over the rise there along the crik bottom."

"Good," said Holy George. "Kid, take a man with you and swing wide to the left and get into position so that you can turn the point down this way when they start pouring up out of their bed ground. We'll swing right and start them. Understand?"

"Sure," said the kid.

"I'll go with him," said Anvil.

Holy George looked at Anvil and then shrugged. "All right, brother, but don't botch this."

"I ain't goin' to botch nothing," said Anvil. "Not this time I ain't."

The kid started off and Anvil rode up beside him. They had nothing to say to each other but occasionally, as they rode slowly forward, they caught each other's eyes and held for an instant.

The kid was watching Anvil in the moonlight, noting the sign of the anvil the man had branded into his tan sombrero band, noting also the identical mark on the butt of the ivory-handled six-gun. Anvil was vain about such things.

They proceeded until they could look down into the dark shadows of the creek bottom. Cottonwoods were masking the herd there, but the click of horn against horn and the occasional scrape of a hoof on rock came to them plainly enough.

"This is the place," said the kid, pulling up.

"Yaw," said Anvil. "This is the place."

The undertone of menace in the man's voice made the kid look at him quickly. Anvil had betrayed more than he knew.

They sat silently, waiting for the first shots. They both knew the plan. Stampede the herd out into the prairie, keep the main body of it moving at a run, let it slow down gradually and then larrup it into the fastnesses of the Little Rockies where the work of changing brands could be done without interruption.

It took Holy George some time to get all the way around. The terrain was rough and silence had to be maintained. The trail crew would still be on guard because of the repeated raidings in other quarters of the range.

"They're taking their time," observed the kid.

Anvil had his palm on the butt of his six-gun. He was staring fixedly at the kid's heart. Anvil was waiting for the first shots from the other side.

"You're acting spooky," said the kid.

"What of it?"

The kid shifted his weight in the saddle and leather creaked. He had a sudden idea and he glanced across the dark bottoms.

"You've been waiting for a long time to get square with me," said the kid.

"Yaw, what of that?"

"Nothing of that except that I think you're too yellow to try anything."

"What?"

"I said a white-livered skunk like yourself could only get a man in the back."

Anvil made an effort to control himself. He felt that he was being driven into something.

"You've been waiting for a chance like this," said the carefully insulting kid. "Your palm's itchin' to be jarred. But you ain't got the nerve. You're yallah straight through, mister. And you're so lowdown a coyote wouldn't gnaw on your carcass if he was starvin' to death. A buzzard wouldn't dirty his feet by lighting on—"

"WHY YOU—"

Anvil yanked at his gun.

The kid dived suddenly to the left, walnut hard and warm in his palm. He fired across his buckskin's neck. The ribbon of flame lashed out to scorch Anvil's half-upraised gun hand.

Anvil pulled the trigger but his shot plowed earth. The ivory-handled gun slid out of his grasp and he clawed at his pommel, coughing. His horse, startled by the deafening shot, was beginning to plunge. Anvil dropped to the sod and lay there, a dark outline against the darker ground.

Instantly other shots crashed across the bottoms and along the rim. Unseen cattle bawled with fright in the cottonwoods. Hoofs rolled thunderously up the slope.

Holy George jutted up out of the blackness and pulled up so hard his mount reared.

"Who fired that shot?" But he was not waiting for the answer. "Get Anvil across his horse! And don't forget his hat! They're after us! Get going!"

Holy George and his riders rolled swiftly by. The kid threw the corpse over the saddle and lashed it there with thongs. Then, carefully, he laid Anvil's hat on a rock with the gun beside it.

He forked leather and tugged at the mount's reins, spurring his own buckskin after the fleeing raiders.

Behind him the hastily assembling trail crew was starting to take up the chase, filling the night with shrill lead and courage-bolstering yip-yeas.

The kid rode with the wind cold upon his young face, trying to tell himself that he had had to do it to keep from getting shot in the back. But even that could not overcome the shock of having killed a man, even break or not.

Anvil's down-dangling hands swatted nervelessly at the bunch grass as his running horse was hauled after the buckskin.

CHAPTER SIX

THE next morning, the Cross G outfit arose nervous and quarrelsome. The cluster of rough shacks which composed the nucleus of the growing spread was carefully protected by two vertical bluffs, and upon these, lookouts were perched surveying the spreading prairie beyond the river.

The kid was sitting outside the bunkhouse, cleaning his six-gun while Holy George paced like an enormous raven up and down the width of the corral.

Holy George stopped. "I still can't see how Anvil could have been such a fool!"

"A man's got to protect himself," said the kid doggedly. "And when it comes to bein' shot in the back, I object."

"But you knew that shot would rouse that camp."

"I told you," said the kid, "that he was all set to plug me in the back and when he drew, could I sit there and take his lead just to keep the camp asleep? It would have been Anvil's shot or mine."

Holy George resumed his pacing. He stopped at the far end of the boot tracks he had made and looked long and narrowly at the kid, his ugly mouth pulled down at the corners and the scar grown purple on his jaw.

He came back. "If I thought you were here just to upset this outfit, I'd drill you like I would a tomato can, brother." He stalked over to his own cabin and went inside. The kid kept on working at his six-gun, the least possible tremor showing in his hand.

A lookout stood up and waved his hat at the ranch. Another rider saw and ran to tell Holy George, who came forth to stand shading his eyes, staring up at the silhouette the scout made against the sky.

"Rider coming," decided Holy George.

They waited nervously until a lone horseman trotted into sight along the dry creek bed which served the ranch as a road. Presently they could see that it was Johnny Simmons.

He must have ridden faster than was his wont, as he was heaving and blowing as hard as his mustang and his fat paunch was going in and out like a bellows.

He got down alongside Holy George.

Holy George turned to his rider. "Call in the lookouts." The man went away on the run.

"George, this is a hell of a thing," puffed Simmons. "Soon as I heard it I rode right out. This is going to put me in a terrible hole and I ain't kidding you."

"What's up?" said Holy George sadly.

"A man from the Circle C rode into town about dawn to get Diehard, and as soon as I heard about it, I went right out and found them in the sheriff's office. I know it's all a mistake, but I want to make sure it don't spread. I got to think of my reputation, George."

"Sure, brother, sure you have."

"This Circle C puncher had a six-gun and a hat with him.

The hat—and this is a fact—had an anvil branded on its band and the six-gun had the same design on it. Where is Anvil Borse?"

"He left us yesterday. Quit because of the kid. You heard him say he was going to quit, and he did. That's all I know about it." Holy George shook his head despondently. "I thought you were removing Diehard Thompson from office."

"I had to wait until Charley Osmond got back from Great Falls and he won't be here until tomorrow."

"Brother," mourned Holy George, "I appreciate this gesture of friendship. The false accusations of Thompson are likely to plant suspicion in the minds of the ranchers around here. And I realize as you do that the finding of this hat and revolver implicates me. However, if a trial—"

"I wouldn't like to see no trial," said Johnny Simmons, scared. "But Diehard is starting the wheels going and there's to be a hearing tomorrow. Of course, nobody believes it except Diehard and nobody will listen to anything he has to say since you made a fool out of him. But still I'd likely get dragged into this and I can't afford it. My reputation—"

"Of course," said Holy George. "And with Diehard out of the way, the hearing won't have any witnesses except a few Circle C boys. My boys all know that Anvil left me yesterday. And I'm shocked to hear he turned rustler. Some of our own stock has been missing, too."

"I wish you could do something," said Simmons.

"I think I can, brother. Won't you come in and have some dinner?"

"No. If you'll give me a fresh horse, I'll start back right away."

"Certainly. Anything to oblige," said Holy George.

"You will do something, won't you?"

"Yes. Of course I will. Do you think I'll let my good name be dragged through the mud? You tell Diehard that I'm coming in to see him at nine tonight and tell him I'll be heeled. He wants his chance and I'll give it to him."

Simmons mopped his brow with relief. A puncher was changing his saddle for him and he started toward the corral.

"If Diehard ain't there," said Simmons, "there won't be much of a hearing. He's been bragging about how he'll nail you the next time he sees you anyway. He claims you got the drop on him by accident."

He mounted and gave Holy George a relieved grin and then rode swiftly down the creek bed and out of sight around the bluff.

The kid had been sitting against the bunkhouse, taking it all in. He expected that something would be said to him about the hat and gun, but Holy George did not so much as glance in his direction as he reentered his cabin.

A short while later, one of the riders came out, whistling carelessly. The kid watched him disappear around the end of a shed and then turned back to watch Holy George's cabin.

The coup was accomplished with ridiculous ease.

Simultaneously, the two scouts appeared on either end of the bunkhouse, rifles pointed at the kid.

Holy George walked sadly out of his cabin.

The kid kept his hands away from his gun and stood carefully up.

"Put him in there," said Holy George. "If this is the way I think it is, I'll attend to him when I get back tonight."

They prodded the kid toward Holy George's cabin, thrust him inside and locked the door.

He stood in the darkened room and heard a gun butt thump as its owner sat down on the steps.

The kid looked around him and then sat down on the edge of the bed, staring at a bearskin rug which sprawled across the floor.

After the first pangs of impotent rage had abated, he got up and paced the walls, looking for a way out.

The situation was not a new one to Lee Beauregarde Thompson. In his younger years, after he had disgraced himself by bulldogging a prize steer or stealing his grandfather's ammunition for practice, he had often been incarcerated in various ranch buildings and he had become accomplished in the science of escape. Even now, with leaden death waiting for him, he could not help but hear the echo of his stern grandfather's voice saying, "Lee! If you don't watch yourself, you'll grow up just like your father!"

He knew his father would not have given up so easily, would not have allowed himself to have been caught so ignominiously. But he had carried on so far. He had to go farther.

The window at the back of the cabin was shuttered tightly. After long study he found a knothole near the middle and he went to work quietly punching it out.

That done, he started the lengthy task of dislodging the outside bar with a nail he had dug out with his fingers and bent with his heel.

He heard Holy George's mustang being led up and he heard the saddle creak as Holy George mounted.

The kid shoved the shutters out into the dusk, looked around and carefully lowered himself to the ground.

A puncher was squatting against the wall not ten feet away. The kid pressed himself back against the building and then began to slide silently toward the unobserving man.

A pebble rolled under his foot. The puncher looked up, startled. He came to his feet with a yell, clawing at his gun.

The kid made the last yard at a leap. He seized the man's wrist and twisted it, slamming a left into the puncher's face.

The gun came free and the kid had it before it touched the ground. The puncher recovered and tried to strike. The kid grabbed his arm and brought the gun butt down on his skull. It was a glancing blow and the man struggled back with a warning yell.

Boots pounded on the other side of the building.

The kid looked around him and dashed the width of the cabin. He turned and sprinted toward the corral. Behind him another puncher came into sight.

The kid flung open the gate just as a shot screamed over his head away from a corral post. The horses within reared and started to mill. One found the opening and dashed forth.

The kid caught his mane and heaved himself up on the mustang's back.

Men were running toward him, firing as they came. The kid hung low under the mount's neck, Indian fashion, without so much as a cinch strap to aid him.

The frightened horse streaked down the dry creek bed. The

kid swung up and sent a warning shot back at the buildings. One Winchester bullet clipped earth under the hammering hoofs and then the ranch was lost to sight.

The kid turned his face toward Wolf River and drummed his heels into the mustang's stretching flanks. The night air whipped the mane and tail out straight and the prairie fled beneath the urgent hoofs.

CHAPTER SEVEN

IT was nine o'clock in Wolf River.

Holy George Gates walked his horse up in front of Long Henry's Place and got slowly down. He took a methodical turn of the reins around the hitch rail and then stepped up to the boardwalk to stand silhouetted in the light from the saloon window, looking like some rusty black bird of prey ruminating on the whereabouts of its next victim.

Troopers and riders and railroad men sidestepped him, as a brawling stream sidesteps a black rock jutting out of its depths.

Holy George stopped a Mill Iron puncher. "I understand, brother, that there's going to be a hearing tomorrow."

"Yeah," said the puncher carelessly. "Old Diehard has got some kind of a loony idea about spotting the rustlers. He's trying to save his face, that's all. It won't come to nothin'." He looked closer at Holy George. "Gee, you come in to shut him up?"

"Thanks, brother."

The puncher moved on and in his wake men stopped and turned and looked at the gaunt, rusty black shadow which was Holy George.

Johnny Simmons waddled up. He was sweating though the night was cold. "It's time you got here. But I think Diehard's run out on you. He disappeared about seven, just after he got

41

your message, and nobody has seen him since. Maybe he's in his room at the Great Northern Hotel."

"I can't let slander stand unchallenged, brother," said Holy George piously.

Simmons swabbed at his brow. "He stirred up a lot of talk but if he ain't at that hearing tomorrow—"

"He won't be at that hearing," said Holy George in an undertaker's voice.

"Good," wheezed Simmons. "I'll be seeing you later."

"Naturally," said Holy George, tentatively touching his hide-out. The .41 was there, as ready and waiting as an updrawn executioner's sword.

The word had spread along the one street of Wolf River. White faces were turned toward Holy George and men stopped to look at him. Belatedly, Wolf River began to remember Diehard's record, much on the order of a discussion among pallbearers around a coffin. But everybody knew that "the pore old devil wouldn't have a chance." Diehard's reputation had vanished on that day when Holy George had not even shot and the respect of the town had gone with the event.

Holy George began to walk down toward the Great Northern Hotel, stiff-legged and cat-eyed, supremely confident, as a wolfhound about to do for a fox terrier.

The light on the street was uncertain, falling in yellow trapezoids upon the boards and dust. It would be hard to spot a target out here in the crazy-quilt night, but Holy George thought his battleground would be a room in the hotel.

He was wrong.

When he was twenty paces from the corner of the hotel, Thompson stepped into shadowy view.

Both men stopped, motionless.

The dusty, battered hat was awry on Thompson's head. The vest flapped a little in the night wind. A faint glitter came from the hammer of the gun slung low on his right side. Another patch of brightness was the star upon his shirt. His shoulders were hunched forward and his arms were dangling, his head thrust forward.

The boardwalk cleared suddenly and, still twenty paces apart, Thompson and Holy George stood their ground.

A tight, expectant group of punchers watched from across the street.

"He come out," whispered one.

"That took nerve."

"He knows it's suicide."

Holy George's doleful tones rumbled in the night. "You know what I come for, Diehard."

Thompson did not speak. He stood there, waiting.

"You been telling the town lies about me," said Holy George slowly. "No man livin' can do that, not even a broken-down wreck like you. Are you going to draw?"

"Draw!" croaked Thompson.

It was too dark to see Holy George's hand move. His coat whipped open and the blunt .41 was heavy in his enormous palm, slashing level for the shot.

Flame streaked from Thompson's waist. Thunder slapped the rickety walls of the canyon of false-fronts. Light flashed from the up-kicking single-action Army.

Deliberately, without waiting to see the effect of his shot, Thompson slid the gun into its holster and turned on his heel.

Holy George was rocking back and forth like a tall tree in a high wind, as though in amazement. His fingers fanned out stiffly and gravity snatched the .41 from his grasp. The hand contracted suddenly.

Holy George started to go down, stiff and jointless. His face hit the splintery boards with a loud, mushy sound.

Though face down, Holy George was laid out for a pious funeral.

Across the street the popeyed crowd stared at the fallen body. Hurriedly they tried to remember the things they had said to taunt Diehard Thompson and, remembering, shivered respectfully. One puncher took off his hat and held it against his chest and gulped, "Jesus!"

Johnny Simmons quaked. As soon as his legs were steady enough to support him he wobbled down the walk to Holy George's horse and crawled urgently into the saddle.

The quirt popped as he brought it down. With a speed which matched his fear in violence, Johnny Simmons sped out of Wolf River toward the Canadian border and possible safety.

When he looked back, Holy George was still staring straight down at the planks with wide, glassy eyes.

Thompson walked up the creaking steps of the Great Northern Hotel and entered the first room on his right. He crossed briskly and turned up the light.

He took off his father's limp and dusty hat and threw it down. He shed his father's vest and star. Lee Beauregarde

Thompson turned and looked at Diehard, trussed up like a hog for market on the sagging bed.

"He's dead," said the kid, taking the gag out of Diehard's mouth and slitting the ropes. "And Johnny Simmons just rolled out of Wolf River forever. And with me as deputy, everything will run as smooth as silk."

But Diehard did not know the whole of it. He sat up, his seamed face scarlet with anger. His old bones fairly rattled under the ferocity of his rage.

"Damn you, you can't do this to me!" shrieked Diehard. "That was *my* fight! Do you think I want to go through the rest of my life knowing that some punk kid had to come up here and fight my battles for me? Do you think I want to know that I'm too old to pull my own gun? I'd rather have gone out there and taken my medicine! Damn you for a meddling young squirt!"

The kid stood back and smiled a little. "There's only one thing you don't know, sir. One thing which makes it all right."

"Nothing could make anything right!"

The kid said, "I'm your son."

Old Diehard gaped. His faded eyes stared. And then, little by little, astonishment left him and he sat slowly back on the bed. He began to swell with pride.

"My son," whispered Diehard.

Hoss Tamer

HOSS TAMER

WHEN the circus went broke, so did Tim Farland. It was an inconvenient place to go broke, Oak Flat, southwest of the Sawtooth Range, where nothing grew that needed water and water didn't exist. The circus was bought at the bankruptcy sale by somebody from St. Louis. The equipment, animals and most of the people went clickety-clacking eastward away from the Great American Desert, turned a bend in the canyon and passed both out of the sight of Tim Farland and out of this story.

Tim stood for a time gazing at the bare place where the big top had stood and then gave his cap a tug and walked into the false-fronted town. At the dry-goods store he found that nobody would buy his clothes.

"Yuh condemned Easterner!" said the crotchety proprietor. "Who'd want them clothes? Nyow if'n you hed yerself a new pair boots—"

"I'm no Easterner," said Tim. "I come from the Hood River country in Oregon, and I train horses. You wouldn't know anybody around here that needs a horse trainer, would you?"

"Bronc buster?" said the proprietor as he picked a decayed tooth. "Well, now, let me see. Seems like . . . Yep. The

Gopher Hole was in here today and he said they had fifty, seventy-five head to whup into shape. That's a spread out south of here, 'leven 'r twelve mile. Mighty tough customers. Boss' name's Randall. Dude Randall. Ain't owned the place long and don't know much about the country but there ain't a bronc buster fer as far as I can think. You really know bronc bustin'? You don't look like it none. No broken bones stickin' out prominent."

While the old man hee-heed about his joke, Tim went out to the livery stable and found himself a bored mustang and a saddle in return for his raincoat. Moths had been at the coat, but the same could be said about the mustang.

Jed Binks, the owner of the stable, a barrel-bellied man with a Fourth of July complexion, looked critically at Tim. "You one of the circus crowd?"

"Was," said Tim.

"I liked them acrobats," said Jed, and he looked at his paunch. "I always wanted to be an acrobat, but look at me!"

Tim grinned. He liked Jed.

"The Gopher Hole may or may not hire you," said Jed. "They're an ornery crowd. Practically every bullet hole you see in my sign up there was fired by Randall's hellions. Well . . . half of them anyway. Dude come to this country under a cloud and when you see him you get scared of bein' struck by its lightnin'. They don't much care who they insults. All lead and whang leather."

"I need a job," said Tim.

Jed looked at the young man's slender height and fresh face. "You must need one pretty bad. If it's just a job, why, I'll give you one cleaning stable. But I couldn't pay more than ten and you sleep in a stall. How come you didn't get a ticket back like the rest of them?"

"Had my own horses and that made me a partner. They took the horses. You can sell those." Tim grinned. "I need money enough to take my ranch out of hock up in Hood River. If I don't make some fast and get it home, they'll be able to use seizure writs for wallpaper, come fall."

"Plunged to buy trick horses and then got tricked," said Jed.

"Yeh. Men ain't near as smart as dumb animals. Any one of my waltzing group could think rings around me, especially when it comes to that low practice they jokingly call high finance. Well, see you around, Mr. Binks."

"Drop in," said Jed. "Whenever you get into town, git down and sit a spell. I like horses."

Tim coaxed the mustang into braving daylight and rode toward the Gopher Hole. What he had told Jed Binks about seizure writs was more than conversation. There was a girl up there, Mary Sims, who had looked awful good to Tim for a long, long time, and if things had gone well this summer she would have been Mrs. Tim Farland. But the sawdust trail hadn't led to wedding bells. Mr. Sims, who had a violent opinion about Farlands, had certainly gotten his wish about this venture.

The Sims patriarch needed a cook and he didn't think a Farland should have a wife to perpetuate the breed. Money in abundance and a thriving ranch would, however, have addled the old man's wits enough to permit Mary to team up. Money was a high type of philosophy to Sims and his objection to Farlands was not so much their liking for fast riding and cards as it was for their lack of bank accounts. There was no point, Sims had said, in losing a good cook just to acquire a son-in-law that could eat.

Entirely beyond Mary was the question of the Farland acres. Hood River country was beautiful; despite the few years it had been settled, the land was already commanding the high price of a dollar and a half an acre, which explained the inevitable seizure writs. Farland's Flying Fox was mostly bottomland and fully a thousand acres of that.

Thinking dolefully on his past and present follies, Tim was not greatly revived by his first glimpse of the Gopher Hole.

The place was run down, fallen down and lying down, with tin cans and garbage liberally landscaping it. There was hardly a sound pole in any one of five corrals and when it rained, if it ever did in this land, it must have been a lot drier outside those shacks than in. Once this had been a tasteful spread with real trees shading a neat fortlike arrangement of buildings. Now the trees were dead and dismembered for firewood and most of the buildings showed no sign of use.

But the gun that covered Tim was no neglected weapon. Its holder stayed behind the rock and said, "Put 'em up and light easy. The first fast play and we'll examine anatomy."

Tim put up his hands and slid off. He was ordered to turn around and it was finally discovered that he was unarmed. As he had no money and had left the bulk of his baggage with Jed, robbery was no motive.

"Now walk slow toward the main house."

Tim walked and found a man there, waiting for him. Dude Randall had tall, bright black gambler's boots and eyes that glittered as opaquely.

"Look what I found," said the sentry. "Rid in without his mama or anybody."

"My name's Tim Farland. I heard you needed a horse trainer. I'm a horse trainer."

"Do tell," said Randall. "A real, live bronc buster. You don't look the part, sonny."

"I'm from Hood River, Oregon. I need a job pretty bad."

"Well, now," said Dude, his wariness relaxing to the point where he let go of his shoulder gun, "maybe we can make a deal at that. Our friend here," he said of the sentry, "was having a little fun. If you can break horses maybe we can make a deal. You in trouble?"

"Well . . ." said Tim, thinking of the circus.

"I savvy," said Dude, thinking of reward posters. "Come along. We got about sixty head that needs a taste of leather."

They walked out toward the horse pasture, the sentry not quite certain yet. In a rickety enclosure of scanty grass, a number of lineback, hammer-headed roans, duns, grays, bays, and in short, various mounts picked thin-ribbedly at the croppings. A few had saddle marks, but most of them looked like something long since passed over by the Digger Indians.

"The army will buy them," said Dude. "They'll give twenty dollars a head if they're broke. I'll give you five dollars a head to break them. How's that?"

Tim wondered why the guard grinned. He looked at the horses and then at Dude. "All right," said Tim. "I'll gentle them up but it will take me a month or so."

"You'll have to do it in a week," said Dude.

"That's impossible," said Tim.

"A week or no deal."

"I'll try," Tim replied, wonderingly.

The sentry let out a yell and three other men appeared. They were bearded and ragtag and it was difficult when you got downwind of them.

One of them hazed out a lineback and another got the main corral gate open. A third quickly roped the mount.

They saddled by means of blindfolding and ear biting, and then the horse stood there, shaking, scared, and ready to go crazy from the pain in his ear.

"What are you trying to do?" said Tim. "That's no way to make a saddler. You lead him around for a couple days and then you work him with the bridle and then a saddle blanket—"

"Ride or no job," said Dude, admiring his dirty fingernails.

Tim wasn't too sure he could do this. He had trained horses for half as many years as he was old and he hadn't forked a wild one twice in the years. And then he thought of the Flying Fox and Mary and thought to himself that old cowpuncher boast, "I can lick that guy, I can kiss that girl, I can ride that bronc and make him whirl—" and so got ready to mount.

They let go before he was fairly in the saddle and then yelled and struck out with quirts.

54

The bronc went crazy. He went straight up and screamed. When he lit, he found he had something on his back and he didn't waste any time deciding it was for decoration.

He went up again and lowered his head to land front-footed with a terrific jar. He reared and whirled and tried to rear back into a gate. Shrieking with rage and terror, he missed the gate. Underestimating the weight on his back he went over too far.

Tim got rid of his stirrups but not quite quick enough. He saw a sky full of flying mane and bronc ears and then a wonderful display of stars.

He didn't know anything for a long time and when he knew it, it wasn't worth finding out.

They'd hauled him to the side of the corral and there he lay in the mud with enough pain in his right shoulder and side to send off skyrockets, ten to a breath.

"He's alive," said somebody without much interest.

"Bronc buster," said another and spat.

"I'm a horse trainer," said Tim but it came out as a groan.

After a little one of the men said, "Charley's goin' in for the mail late this afternoon."

"I wasn't goin' to use the wagon," said Charley.

"People would talk," said Dude. "Use the wagon and take him in to the doctor—when you get around to it. Where's that bottle, Jake? I laughed so hard, I'm hoarse."

They put him into a buckboard, omitting straw, when it got cool enough to make comfortable driving, and Charley went off in the obvious belief that he was driving a stagecoach.

The road being what it was, the springs what they were and the hardness of the boards together mercifully put Tim to sleep before a mile had been traveled.

Out of this nightmare he would sometimes emerge to fancy that he was hellbound with the devil for a driver and he would try to speak to the demon on the seat to find out if repentance had to have quite so much punishment right at the start, and then the sky would red out and turn black again.

There was not much left of Tim Farland when the buckboard hauled up at the Wells Fargo building. Charley yelled up to the second floor, "Hey Doc! Got a feller here with a complaint!"

After a long time, a man came down the side stairs in his shirt sleeves and peered at Tim. "My gosh! What have you been doing?" the doctor yelled at the unworried Charley. "This man is badly injured!"

"We was out of straw," said Charley.

"Help me lift him out!" said the doctor, his fat cheeks puffing in and out with rage.

"Lifted him in," said Charley, unperturbed.

The doctor turned to the gathering crowd on the walk. "Give me a hand, you loafers." He steadied Tim's head as they lifted him out but Tim blanked again.

The doctor, being German and very thorough, then told the driver exactly what he thought of him and followed Tim's bearers up the stairs. It didn't bother Charley. He clucked to his lathered horses and moved off.

There ensued a most enlightening piece of bone setting, the little German discovering that two ribs and the collarbone were greensticked. Tim was out during the best part of it, but very much awake during the worst, awake enough to bite the teeth stick half in two.

It was many a day before Tim was entirely sane about what had happened to him. He lay in the doctor's small "hospital" and tried to piece together the events. It hurt to think about them, but he had to. Word by word, the conversation of Dude and his men was patched into proper—or improper—order and there began to be born in Tim Farland something which had never been there before: a terrible hunger. A hunger for human blood, all of it from the Gopher Hole and all the Gopher Hole had to give him.

He would awake from nightmares fighting his bronc and the bronc was Dude Randall wearing Charley's hat and he was almost ready to saddle break Dude when somebody would drive a flaming arrow into his side and make him fall off.

"There, there," said the doctor one night. "Pretty soon you get up out of this and you feel pretty good. You're young. You got nightmares but you'll get over them. Now get some sleep and forget all this nonsense about shooting gophers."

But Tim didn't get over the desire to eat gopher meat. When he could finally hobble around, his shoulder in splints, he borrowed a gun off the doctor, who had collected several in the way of services to the deceased, and tried to practice drawing. But he didn't seem to be able to do much with his good left hand. Not with a gun. He brooded over it.

Jed Binks came to the "hospital" one day and turned his cap around until one would have thought the floor would become soaking wet. "Tim, I been thinking."

Tim got ready to dodge an offered loan.

Jed scratched his fat belly and tried to grin. "Tim, I got my poor old mother over in 'Dobe Junction and she's awful sick. I figure maybe I better go over and see her for a few days. Do you think as a favor to me—and a dollar a day and keep—you could look after my livery stable?"

Tim got ready to refuse but Jed wouldn't wait. "I'm in a terrible hurry, Tim. My hoss is waitin' outside. I leave you in charge and the flour's in the right-hand drawer and Bill Mullin ain't paid for last night— Goodbye!"

Tim went down and looked over his new responsibility. He was not very amazed to learn that Jed had gone off on a deer hunting trip to kill time and he was not very much startled, three days later, to find Jed back again.

But every time Tim tried to quit, Jed would get quick-tempered over having his thoughts interrupted and Tim finally stopped trying to bring it up. A week later, Tim was an accepted fixture of the Star Livery Stable.

It was pretty hard to wield a fork with one hand but Tim managed to sneak through the cleaning job whenever Jed didn't catch him. It was easier to feed the horses after Jed widened the mow steps so you only needed one hand. But it didn't take any manual dexterity whatever to beat Jed at checkers three nights out of four after the horses were bedded down and Oak Flat was in full, riotous swing.

It was early August that the Gopher Hole crowd came to spend almost every night in town. There was an evident reason for this in Mrs. Bondell's new waitress and a less evident one in the mine payroll and yearly bonus which was due one of these nights to come in on the Transcontinental and repose until delivered in the Wells Fargo safe.

Jed talked about it and then talked about it more when the Gopher Hole crowd took to living at the New York Hotel, stabling their mounts at the livery stable.

They were good horses. And each saddle had a roll tied behind it and a full water bottle hanging from the horn. Dude Randall had ordered a good feed of corn to be given them every night and the horses, getting no exercise during the day, were uncomfortably lively.

"You sure you want to keep stuffin' good corn down their ornery throats?" said Jed. "Them five cayuses will kick this place apart!"

Randall gave him a veiled smile. "I treat my horses right, Binks. But it wouldn't be no loss if they did—so far as I can see." And Dude stood with shining boots and shiny eyes and looked contempt around him. He saw Tim.

"There's the hoss tamer!" said Randall.

Tim glared but kept his mouth shut.

"I wouldn't go near them there mounts of mine, dearie," said Randall. "They're nasty!"

Charley laughed at the door and Randall left.

Tim hefted the pitchfork he was holding. He had a lot of misery in his heart these days, what with thinking of the Flying Fox about to fly away from him forever and Mary's blue eyes bent over her pappy's cookstove.

"No, you don't," said Jed. "Smack lead into a man face to face and it's legal. But they frown on pitchforks. Come on in and let me beat you at checkers."

Usually Tim said, "You couldn't beat nobody," and proved it. Tonight he said, "I got work to do," and went on forking hay.

Jed, in the following days, began to worry about his friend. The boy wasn't eating well. He was thinking too much. Why, he even walked in his sleep.

Tim took to meeting the Transcontinental Flier. He made friends with the Wells Fargo clerk—despite Jed's jealousy. Tim played checkers with the Upland Stage driver every day. And he began to hang around Mrs. Bondell's greasy spoon though, as Jed said, one whiff of that cooking would poison a rattlesnake. The Gopher Hole crowd jostled Tim mentally and physically when they could and started the whole town calling Tim the "Hoss Tamer." Tim took it. He played his checkers and met the train and endlessly discussed the dusty condition of the weather with the Wells Fargo man.

And the weeks went on. Soon it would be possible for Tim to wear a sling and shuck the splints and he ceaselessly worked his right hand to keep it limber.

Jed petulantly wrote by dictation Tim's letters to Mary and cussed over spelling and then eagerly wanted to hear what Mary's letters had in them in return. A bird with a sharp call had taken residence in the place, and Jed added his own speculations in the letters, with his own news.

Tim took walks between tending horses and one day Jed complained to him, "You smell like furrin' whiskey. What you been doin'?"

"Aniseed," said Tim noncommittally. "It makes good liniment. Grows on bushes."

"It shore smells strong as mustang liniment. Maybe stronger.

But I figure if you rubbed down a hoss with that stuff his rider'd have a lot of fights about wearin' perfume."

"It's an herb," said Tim. "It's good for a lot of things." And then he pushed out the board. "How about some checkers?"

Jed forgot about it in the strain of trying to figure out why Tim could always get four jumps in rotation that way, and Tim never brought it up again.

Tim continued with his routine. Oak Flat slumbered in the broil of late summer. The train was late or otherwise. Jed kept losing. And the mounts of the Gopher Hole crowd grew very sleek.

And then one night Tim came back from the station looking catlike. He stopped off at Wells Fargo and found the agent and the sheriff very busy. He was not welcome and he continued on to the livery stable.

At nine o'clock Dude Randall came over and said he figured him and the boys would go back to the ranch late tonight and he'd appreciate having the horses saddled and ready in front of the New York Hotel about eleven.

Jed took the gold pieces for horse keep and grumbled back to saddle the rearing and restive mounts. "Eleven, heck. I'm gettin' rid of these demons afore they make matchsticks out'n my stable. You keep away, Tim. This is no place for a man with a bad wing."

Tim stayed away and, considerably before the hour, the mounts were hauling and tugging at their reins before the hotel.

Tim went back to see how things went at Wells Fargo. Two or three citizens greeted him as "Hoss" and he nodded in a preoccupied way. He found the building barred, but through a slit in the iron shutters he saw the clerk, back to the safe, a shotgun across his knees.

The sheriff and two deputies were in the Longchance Saloon playing stud with Dude Randall. Obviously the sheriff wanted to be handy and intended to stay up late. Dude was willing to assist him. Watching the game languidly were Dude's four punchers.

The place was not very safe, Tim decided, and he left early. But he didn't retire. He sat with the back of his chair tipped against the livery stable door and kept watch on the Longchance.

The town grew wilder and then began to calm. It must be around one, Tim decided, glancing at the stars.

He must have dozed for a moment, for he did not see Charley, the hand who had driven him to town in the wagon, leave the Longchance. The faint moonlight disclosed him in the middle of the road, heading for Wells Fargo. Charley was carrying something. He lit a match. He threw.

The trail of sparks hissed. Tim removed himself around the corner. There was a swelling flash and an air-crushing boom. Smoke rolled hysterically up from the Wells Fargo porch.

Tim hadn't counted on that, and he was a little stunned. He saw Sheriff Bainsly rush out to the porch with his deputies. They halted there, halted long enough. Three men struck them from behind with three gun butts and they went down. One deputy was not out. He rolled and tried to draw and was pinned to earth with lead.

Tim was too deaf to hear the shot. He saw the flash. Saw

other flashes and then Dude and his men were at the Wells
Fargo door, kicking through. They retreated for an instant
and there was another explosion. When they came out the
second time, they were carrying heavy sacks and they ran
through the night-gray dust with difficulty.

A rifle whammed up the street. Tim's hearing was better
now. He heard one of the Gopher Hole men yell, saw him
fall and writhe. Charley picked up his sacks and kept going.

The restive mounts would barely permit the loading of
sacks, tied neck to neck. But Dude, Charley and two others
were quickly up. The rifle whammed again, a buffalo gun. It
jolted Charley but he kept his saddle.

"Let's go!" roared Dude, firing into the upstreet darkness.

The mounts reared and started to run. They lengthened
their strides under quirts and rowels and they passed the Star
Livery Stable, the riderless one following after.

Tim stood in plain sight. He put his fingers in his mouth
and blew a piercing, compelling note.

Five horses veered and reared. They fought and pawed air
and they lunged straight toward Tim.

Tim had thought the door behind him was open. It was
not. The first horse, startled forward by spurs and curses,
struck him and he fell. The unmanageable mounts screamed
and reared and fought, hoofs striking inches away from Tim.

His breath was gone but he got to the knob. The door
opened and he was inside and Jed's scatter-gun was out of
the corner. Tim whistled again.

The horses lunged as though they were trying to enter the
door. Their crazed riders fought and yelled.

The unmanageable mounts screamed and reared and fought, hoofs striking inches away from Tim.

Dude snapped a shot which fanned Tim's cheek and the scatter-gun, carefully aimed to miss horses, flamed with authority. Dude reeled.

The second barrel went. Charley lifted out of his saddle. The rifle whammed twice, close range now, and the Wells Fargo shotgun blazed.

Two riders went down.

And then there was peace. Tim had swung open the main door and the horses were inside.

Charley was alive but that would be remedied, for the deputy was dead. Dude didn't look pretty, but he would never mind a thing like that where he was now.

The sheriff was confused.

"What did you do?" he demanded of Tim. "All of a sudden them horses was hightailing it for nowhere and then they come around and tried to climb a wall. What did you do?"

"Whistled to 'em," said Tim.

"That's a fact," said the Wells Fargo man. "I heard him."

"I seen him!" said the deputy.

"That's nerve," said somebody. "Why, he was like to be kilt!"

"Shore he whistled," said Jed. "Ain't he the best hoss trainer in the hull danged world? When he whistles, they come!"

"There'll be rewards," said the sheriff, "and I reckon you got 'em comin' after the fool trick I played. Guess I ought to a knowed."

"Wells Fargo will pay a thousand and that's above what wanted men will be worth," said the clerk, rubbing a bruised and powder-stained cheek.

"You get to my office," said the puffing little doctor. "I knew

I saved that Farland hoss tamer for a reason." The crowd went away, not so much to remove the debris from the ground, but to talk about it comfortable and prideful over bottles. Jed gave the doctor a last bit of help, and saw Charley borne off and then scattered dust on the wet spots. He tagged in after Tim.

Jed looked carefully around. "Tim, how'd you bewitch them danged hosses?"

Tim unloaded the aniseed into the stove. He didn't need it now. And he didn't need these other weeds now either. A queer riot of odor filled the room.

"Herbs," he said. "Horses go loco around certain smells and this time they connected one with that whistle. They shoulda been exercised," he added drily.

"I heard it many a time. I thought it was a bird."

"It was the bird all right," said Tim. But he wasn't thinking about what he was saying. He was thinking about the Hood River country and one Mary Sims. Still thinking, he went on up the street to where they were demanding the right to drink to the greatest horse trainer in the world.

The Ghost Town
Gun-Ghost

CHAPTER ONE

POKEY MACKAY awoke from his customary doze and gave the desert to the east a startled stare. He had been sitting on the porch of the New Yorker Hotel, which was directly opposite the Palace Saloon, where he could keep the entire Main Street of Pioneer under the required surveillance. But now he came down off the porch with a stiff-legged gait and stood in the thick, untrodden dust of the street to squint his watery blue eyes and pull at his straggly walrus mustache. From his pocket, he extracted a rusty sheriff's star and pinned it on his dingy black vest. Then he changed his mind and put the star back in his pocket.

"Look there, Danny," said Pokey Mackay to the empty air. "Looks as though we're goin' to have visitors."

"Looks like you're right, Pokey," returned Pokey Mackay. "You got the sharpest eyes I ever see! What do you s'pose he's doin' in these parts?"

"Well," replied Pokey Mackay, "there's nothin' like givin' him the greetin' proper to a newcomer to the metropolis of Pioneer. See you later, Danny." And so saying, he limped up the shack-lined Main Street, leaving little whirls of dust where his run-over boots made prints.

Still small on the desert, a man was making his way between

yucca and century plants. It was obvious that the stranger had a game leg, for each time he changed his course, the faulty limb threatened to cave, but this evident ailment received scant attention. The stranger halted every hundred yards and turned around to shield his eyes against the sun and peer intently down the trail as though he watched for pursuit. The reason he walked found answer in the dusty saddle he dragged by the horn and the battered bridle he carried over his arm. Most striking of all was the complete absence of a hat—for this lack under the desert sun was extremely dangerous. The ragged jeans were turned far up from the high-heeled boots and, all in all, the stranger appeared to be a very shoddy individual—that is, all except for the two guns which defiantly hurled back the sun's rays with each faltering step.

A hundred yards from the edge of the ghost town the visitor stopped and gave the city limits sign a long study. Then, probably because of the rattlesnake which was coiled about the post, the cracked lips parted in a brief grin. And the grin widened when he caught sight of the waiting Pokey Mackay.

"Howdy," greeted Pokey. "Welcome to Pioneer."

"Howdy," was the reply. "You don't happen to have anything to drink in this city, do you?"

Pokey extended a hand which the stranger shook doubtfully. "Sure we got plenty to drink. That is, if you don't want no fancy stuff like crème de coca."

The stranger gave Pokey a brief scrutiny and then grinned again. "I didn't mean redeye. I'm too broke for any of that. I meant water."

Pokey Mackay took the stranger's arm and began to steer him in the direction of the Palace Saloon. "Y'don't have to worry none about that. The barkeep over there at the Palace is a friend of mine." Then Pokey stopped abruptly and looked at the twin .45s which graced the stranger's hips. "Y'ain't a gunman, are you?"

The other's gray eyes flicked open with surprise and then narrowed. For a moment, Pokey was favored with a chill stare and he shifted uncomfortably.

"I didn't mean nothin' by it," pleaded Pokey. "I just got to be careful, that's all. The sheriff is awful perticular about gunmen since the other crowd came through here last week."

"The other crowd?" The gray eyes were even narrower. "What other crowd?"

Pokey shifted his weight and wriggled in the voluminous folds of the black frock coat. Then his watery blue gaze hardened and his face became a shade redder. "Bunch of damned varmints came chasin' through here a mile a minute and shot up the Wells Fargo office and drunk up a lot of liquor without payin' for it! Five of them, they was. The sheriff and mayor was awful peeved about it."

"I reckon they would be at that," replied the stranger with a smile. "Now let's get the drink."

The Palace Saloon was held together solely by grace of its reputation. The rickety false front sagged on one side, the porch was empty of many planks, and the swinging doors swung no more. Inside, the dust on the floor was a full inch thick and quite undisturbed save for a narrow path along the battered bar and in front of the stacked bottles.

"Barkeep!" said Pokey to the empty room, slapping on the bar as he spoke. "Barkeep! Set 'em up."

The stranger gave a start, looked quickly about and then goggled at Pokey. But Pokey, without batting an eye, stepped quickly around between the mahogany and the murky mirrors and pulled a towel around his waist.

"Howdy, gents," said Pokey. "What'll it be? Redeye?"

With a sudden grin, the stranger placed a foot on the dark brass rail. "Yes, I reckon that'll be all right. Four fingers for me."

Pokey polished up two glasses and then uncorked a huge bottle which he set on the bar. This done, he removed the apron and quickly slid around to the outside. "Jimmy," he said with a glance at the newcomer, "I'd like to have you meet Mr. . . . Mr. . . ." then to the stranger, "What did you say your name was?"

Batting his eyes rapidly, the stranger managed to close his mouth and say, "Ross Delavan. That's the name."

"Yes, Jimmy," continued Pokey Mackay, "this is Mr. Delavan." Solemnly, he picked up the bottle and poured out a drink for himself, indicating that Ross Delavan should follow suit.

"Charge it up," Pokey ordered the mythical Jimmy. He then took Delavan's arm and piloted him to the doorless door back to the silent street. "Now, Mr. Delavan, I'm going to take you down and introduce you to the Wells Fargo agent in case you have any valuables you want stored."

Together they walked through the dust toward a wearily listing board shack which bore the legend, crookedly lettered, "Wells Fargo. Gold Agents. Mail." Delavan hitched at the saddle he still dragged and limped along with a wondering grin on his face.

Inside, Pokey released Delavan's arm and spoke straight at an empty swivel chair beside a roll-top desk. "Benny, this is Mr. Delavan, a stranger to the place. Mr. Delavan, this is Benny. If you want to store any valuables, Benny'll put them in his safe over there." Pokey jerked his thumb at a rusty iron box in the corner whose door was tightly shut and bolted. Then, without a second's warning, Pokey swooped down on the chair and placed his boots on the desk amid the dust.

"Glad to know you," greeted Pokey. "If you're a friend of Pokey Mackay's, you're a friend of mine. I'm terrible sorry I can't stow anything in that safe for you, but a flock of varmints stormed in here a couple weeks ago and closed the danged thing on me and I haven't been able to open it since. Goin' to be here long?"

"Oh," said Delavan. "That all depends on the business conditions around here." His gray eyes twinkled and he sat down on an empty box.

"Wall, business ain't so good these days. Seems like money is pretty tight. But things is pickin' up around here. Just yesterday, Pokey here discovered a billion-dollar gold mine." Pokey jerked his head at the place where he had stood a moment before. "Discovered the thing right up the street a ways. Gold layin' all over the place about three feet thick. You don't even have to pan it, it just jumps into your poke."

Delavan grinned again at the little man who had now removed the black hat from his shiny bald head and was busily fanning himself with it.

73

Pokey Mackay suddenly shed his lazy air and started forward with bugging eyes which stared at the floor beside Delavan's feet. "Holy Smoke!" exclaimed Pokey. "I must have dropped that out of my last pay envelope!"

Delavan glanced down, not expecting to see anything, but then he, too, stared and his gray eyes went cold as they narrowed. He was looking at a packet of shiny new bills which lay fresh in the dust, their wrapper quite undisturbed. Reaching swiftly down, he picked up the sheaf and glanced out of the corner of his eye at the startled Pokey, hefting the bills as he did so. Then, with a swift change of expression, Delavan handed the bills to the little man, sighing deeply as he did so.

Pokey smiled importantly. "I get awful careless with my pay. Y'see, I can charge everything I want to in town—I'm that well known—and I get careless. Y'see, I never even missed this pack of a thousand dollars. I'm that careless." He shook his head slowly over his own wickedness and then got to his feet, still counting the money. "I'm gettin' pretty much behind on my bills hereabouts, and while I got this money handy, I reckon I'll scoot around and get all paid up."

Delavan frowned and opened his mouth to speak—then he shut it with a tight click and got up from the box to follow Pokey Mackay back into the brassy sunlight of the silent street.

Back on the porch of the New Yorker Hotel, Pokey turned to Delavan. "You might as well quit cartin' that saddle around and put up here for the night. This is the best place in town and I reckon you'll find it just right."

With a glance up and down the Main Street, which was

empty of other hostelries, Delavan followed Pokey inside and smiled narrowly as he watched his new friend go through all the conversation of paying his bill.

"Here is the three hundred I owe you," Pokey told the empty air on the other side of the counter. "That pays me up and a month in advance."

After he had quickly rounded the counter's end, Pokey said, "Thank you, Mr. Mackay. You're one of our best customers and I'm certainly glad to have you with us. If the gentleman with you wants a room, we'll give him the best in the house." And Pokey took the money and stuffed it back in his coat pocket.

Ross Delavan laid his saddle down in the corner of the bare-walled room and sat down on the lath bed among a swirl of dusty quilts to watch Pokey Mackay disappear down the stairway at the end of the corridor. Delavan watched through the broken window until he saw the other appear in the dusty street and walk across to a building which was decorated with a lamp black sign which said "Sheriff" and which had an age-yellowed reward poster tacked beside the door.

Assured that he would be alone for a few minutes, Ross Delavan unbuckled the heavy .45s and draped them over the foot of the bed. Then he rolled up one leg of his jeans until his knee was exposed and slowly examined a blood clot which bulged blackly out from the kneecap, and which centered a long crease. He whistled slightly as he touched the crease and his dark face tightened with pain. The wound began to bleed and Delavan looked quickly about to see if he could find anything which would serve as a bandage. Failing in his search he pulled out his shirttail and tore a long strip from its bottom.

With the strip held in his hand, Delavan limped out of the door and down the corridor until he came to a door whose knob was bright. Cautiously he opened it and stepped inside to find that he stood in Pokey Mackay's bedroom.

The bed was neatly made and the floor was well swept. Against the wall stood several rifles—Henrys, Sharps and Winchesters—and these drew Delavan swiftly across the room. With a quick flip of his wrist he looked into the breech of a Sharps and extracted the cartridge. He turned the oversize bullet in his hand. A glance was sufficient to see that age had robbed the cartridge of its use. Placing the rifle back among its fellows, Delavan stepped to a bureau which was heaped with newspapers.

The *Pioneer Herald* topped the first page of the upper sheet and Delavan's eyes bugged as he read a dateline fifteen years old. The newspaper was filled with the news of a new gold strike far to the north and at the bottom of the page, a banner proclaimed that this was positively the last issue of the mighty *Pioneer Herald.* That, for Delavan, solved the mystery of the deserted town. He knew now that the place had been lacking in population for many, many hot years, and that Pokey Mackay . . .

But beside the stack of printed sheets lay a newer pile of hand-lettered newspapers. The sheets were arranged in sequence and the oldest dateline began a month after the original journal had ceased publication. This oldest sheet bore the headline: "Pokey Mackay Elected Mayor of Pioneer." And one by one, up through an endless chain of days, came stories of the prowess and depredations of Pokey Mackay. Elections, one after another, all unanimous in their vote, brought Benny and Jimmy and Harry and Dick into office, and the first paragraph of every story always mentioned Pokey Mackay.

Delavan's smile was sympathetic as he turned back to the room and picked up a bottle of whiskey from a box beside the bed. As he daubed the liquor on the wound with the cloth, the pain of stinging alcohol did not rob his face of the smile.

Late in the afternoon, Delavan awoke from a troubled sleep to hear the sound of hoofbeats coming down the street. He raised up on one elbow and snatched at his guns which he buckled around him. Then, crouched, his face cold with expectancy, he sidled to the broken window and looked down, his hands taut on the butts of the twin .45s.

A thickset man, astride a buckskin mustang, galloped around the corner of the Palace Saloon and abruptly drew rein in the center of Main Street. Against the newcomer's checkered shirt glittered a polished star, and the expression on the rough-hewn face gave the world to understand that here was the law after its legal prey.

Delavan drew out his right-hand gun and spun the cylinder, his eyes chill as he contemplated the shot. Then a cheery voice came through the silence of the town and Delavan saw Pokey Mackay come out of the sheriff's office and walk to the side of the newcomer.

"Howdy!" greeted Pokey. "Y'ain't been around for pretty near a year. Get down and have a drink. How is Batsville gettin' along?"

"Gettin' along all right," growled the newcomer with a glance at the surrounding buildings. "The drink sounds good." And, leaving his bronc tethered to the breeze, he walked with Pokey to the door of the Palace Saloon.

When the pair below had disappeared through the doorless door, Delavan cautiously slipped down the stairs and went out the back of the New Yorker Hotel. Skirting the rickety buildings, he made his way far up the street and then dashed across the open to hover for an instant in the shelter of a doorway. He eyed the newcomer's horse with a puzzled frown as though half-minded to make a break for it. Then he turned and crept along until he found the back door of the Palace Saloon.

Inside there was a lonesome clink of glass which was followed by a loud hiccup.

Then came the voice of Pokey Mackay. "Pardon me. I get careless of my manners, these days."

"Uh-huh," replied the other. "Now I want some information. What happened to that varmint I trailed in here?"

"What varmint?" queried Pokey.

"You know who I mean," growled the newcomer. "The guy with the game leg lugging his saddle. I found his dead horse out in the desert and I trailed him right on in. And," his voice dropped a note, "I saw by the footprints where you went out to meet him. Now, where is he?"

"Just a minute, Purcell," said Pokey, "even if I had seen this feller, it wouldn't be your job to take him away. You ain't got no authority in this town at all. I'm sheriff here, and I was duly elected as such by popular vote. That's more than I can say for you."

"Don't try that one on me, Pokey," growled Purcell. "I'm on to you. This feller robbed a bank, that's what he did. And he shot three men doing it, too, and them all bein' bystanders."

"How do you know he done it?" asked Pokey.

"Because a feller seen him, that's how! And before the cashier died he must of shot this feller in the knee. You don't have to tell me my business, Pokey Mackay, and you can drop those funny tricks around me, too. You ain't got any right to that sheriff's badge and you know it damned well!"

Pokey's voice was very even when he replied. "That's plenty of that, Mr. Purcell. As mayor of Pioneer I order you out of the city limits. If you don't go, I'll have the sheriff and his deputies kick you out."

"For God's sake! Pokey," cried Purcell, "spare me that hokum and tell me where this gent is hangin' out!"

"Get out of town," ordered Pokey. "I deport you as an undesirable alien!"

Delavan, cautiously peering through the crack in the back door saw the two standing face to face in the dusty, dim interior of the saloon. He tensed as he saw Purcell raise his fist and shake it in Pokey's face.

"Do you want a taste of this?" howled Purcell.

For answer, Pokey stepped back and handed his visitor a

right to the jaw. Purcell's head moved a fraction of an inch, and then, like a charging bull, the sheriff rushed at Pokey, arms flailing, eyes distorted with anger.

Pokey tried to stand up to the hail of blows but he was forced back against a rickety gambling table. With a splintering crash the wood gave and Pokey fell heavily into the dust, which rose about him in a cloud.

Pressing his advantage, Purcell stepped in with heavy boots and gave Pokey a solid kick in the ribs. Then Mackay was up again, trodding heavily on the creaking planks, trying to exchange blow for blow with a man twice his weight.

The stirred dust rose and eddied about the fighters until nothing could be seen but dim shadows weaving back and forth and Delavan was unable to distinguish one from the other.

Silently, Delavan entered on tiptoe, skirting the bar and tables—coming, with each step, closer to the combatants, obscured by the choking fog. For an instant, Purcell loomed up, a tremendous, straining bulk, and Delavan stepped closer. With a quick right to the sheriff's body followed by a shattering left to the stubbly jaw, Delavan stepped back out of sight to see Purcell skid back across the slivery planks and bring up under a table. Then, unperceived by either of the warriors, Delavan jumped back and resumed his first position outside the back door.

Gradually the dust settled and Pokey crawled to his feet, dusting himself off with nervous hands. Grimly he peered about the room, his round face red with exertion, his gray walrus mustache turned yellow with the dry fog. At last he saw the unconscious Purcell lying in a doubled-up position, and he rapidly blinked his watery blue eyes.

With all the pent-up fury of a terrier, Pokey jumped to Purcell's side and picked the man up by his shoulders to dump him in a shivering chair.

"Wha-wha-what hit me?" quavered the sheriff, feeling his face tenderly. He looked up and saw Pokey.

"You get out of this town!" cried Pokey Mackay. "And don't lose no time doin' it either. Get, or I'll smack you again!"

Purcell looked at the doubled fist which was being shaken in front of his face and then up at the round face, disbelief in his usually hard eyes. But he rubbed his jaw again and then, without a word, dived for the front door of the saloon and loped toward his cayuse.

Pokey bellowed loud into the dust which came from the horse's flying hoofs and again shook his fist. "And don't never come back!"

Delavan grinned from behind the saloon at the retreating Purcell's back, for it was obvious that the man took Pokey's threat to heart.

Pokey, still dusting himself and strutting, met Delavan in front of the New Yorker Hotel. "You shoulda seen that scrap!" bubbled Pokey. "That he-critter was after a young feller I seen a couple days ago and when I told him I wouldn't turn my prisoner over to no feller that didn't have no jurisdiction on these premises, he got nasty—awful nasty—and I had to knock him cold. That's what I did, too. Knocked him colder'n a iceberg. I guess he knows who's sheriff of this town!"

"Yes, sir!" agreed Delavan with a grin. "I reckon he does at that."

"I ain't surrenderin' no prisoners to nobody! Want to see my prisoner?" Pokey, with no further prologue, started toward the sheriff's office.

Delavan gaped a moment and then smiled. In the sheriff's office, he stood before a bedraggled cell at the back and smiled anew.

Pokey addressed the bars. "Feelin' all right, young feller? That's fine. We'll have your trial in a few days and I may be able to let you off."

"Doesn't look like no criminal," remarked Delavan.

"No," replied Pokey with a judicious shake of his bald head. "To tell the truth, Mr. Delavan, I don't think he's guilty."

Delavan followed Pokey back into the front of the building and watched the little man settle himself in a chair behind the scarred desk.

With a smile, Pokey continued, "We'll have a trial in a few days. Yes, sir, we'll have the greatest trial you ever heard of! Y'see, this young feller's accused of bank robbery. Seems like he bored three fellers while he was doin' it, too. Right across the street there is where it happened. Right in that Wells Fargo office. But a feller with a mother like he's got can't be guilty of no such crime."

Startled anew, Delavan gasped, "Mother?"

"Sure," returned Pokey with a serious nod toward the door. "The little lady we just seen goin' out is his mother. Didn't she look sweet, though? Hit pretty hard by this trial business, too. Costs money to hire lawyers and such."

Delavan's eyes narrowed and grew chill. "What happened to all the money?"

"The money?" Pokey's expression went blank and then his face lit up. "Oh, yes. The money. Well, sir, don't believe it if you won't, but we got every penny of that there money right back in the Wells Fargo safe. Thousands and thousands of dollars it was. Want to see it?"

Without changing his expression, Delavan followed Pokey down to the Wells Fargo office and entered, watching Pokey kneel in front of the iron box and fumble with the bolts.

"Damn it!" cried Pokey, still kneeling and fumbling. "Them fellers that come in here some time ago went and jammed this thing all up! Never will be able to get it open now!" He stood up and mopped at his forehead with a bandanna. "Reckon we'll have to get us some dynamite. Ain't that right, Jimmy?" With a weary smile in the direction of the empty swivel chair, Pokey walked out.

A shiver had gone up and down Delavan's spine as he saw the empty chair, for his imagination was playing tricks on him and he had confidently turned to the seat, fully expecting to see the Wells Fargo agent.

CHAPTER TWO

I N the cool of a desert morning a week after his arrival in Pioneer, Delavan heard a jumble of voices which seemed to come from far down the single dilapidated street. As Pokey Mackay and Delavan were the only two inhabitants of the ghost town, Delavan jumped out of bed, pulled on his guns and then his boots and thrust a worried face through the glassless window of his room. Then he relaxed.

A shifting mass of ponies stood saddleless along the hitchrail of the building marked "Trading Post" and it needed no second glance to inform Delavan that these were the property of Hopi Indians. The redskins themselves were within the trading post, leaving a medley of bawling papooses and gossiping squaws in the sunshine of the street.

Pulling the hat Pokey had given him down over his high forehead, Delavan went down the stairs and out to pick his way through the bedlam of the sidewalk.

The interior of the trading post was crammed with color and sound, and in the thick of it, important behind the counter, was Pokey Mackay, bargaining with blackhaired braves. On the counter lay a weird assortment of patched saddles, faded cloth, piled brass and copper bolts, battered hats, iron hammers, worn shoes, broken clocks, torn coats, and, in short, a complete array of the things one would expect to find scattered about in a ghost town.

Pokey looked up and saw Delavan enter and placed a momentary halt to his bargaining. "My friends," said Pokey in a half-Hopi jargon to the crowd at large, "this is my friend Governor Selfridge. I want you to shake hands with him and say 'How!'"

Delavan looked at Pokey for an instant and then at the Indians who had immediately begun to swarm about him. One by one he shook their hands.

Pokey said, "I was tellin' them that you'd come out just to see them, Governor. They been gettin' sort of disrespectful, lately."

And so Delavan solemnly nodded at each and every brave and pumped grimy hands until his wrist was tired. His face was settling into a mask of weariness when the last and mightiest warrior of them all—to judge from his bearing and voice—came up and put out his hand.

Delavan caught sight of the Indian's waist as he held the fingers. There he saw a new Colt .45, ivory handled in its holster fastened to the bullet-studded belt. His eyes grayed and became brittle. It was strange enough to see an Indian packing a revolver, but this particular gun had a certain marking on the butt.

In a strange, taut monotone, Delavan asked, "Where did you get that gun?"

The Indian stepped back, his face expressionless. "Me buy."

"Go easy," continued Pokey.

"No," corrected Delavan. "You didn't buy that gun. It doesn't mean anything to me where you got it." He managed a smile, though his eyes were still icy. "I'm your friend."

"You're the governor!" amended Pokey.

With the word *governor,* the Indian's face again became mobile and he displayed his white teeth. He extracted the .45 and held it, butt first, toward Delavan, who took it quickly.

"Me find," said the Indian. "Me find on dead man in desert three smokes north. He shot here," and he placed a significant finger between his eyes.

"Thanks," smiled Delavan, returning the gun.

"Now," cried Pokey in the jargon. "What am I bid for this brass vase?" And he held up a cuspidor.

The trading went on for an hour and then, with loud shouts, the Indians mounted and rode away, certain that they had mercilessly fleeced the trader.

Pokey came out of the ramshackle building and locked the door with a huge iron key. He walked up to where Delavan waited. "Well, Billy got us enough jerked meat and candied cactus and chicory and roots and tobacco to last us a month."

Delavan's eyes were far away, but now they came back to the present with a start. He could never quite accustom himself to the numerous mythical people who existed in the town. "Oh, Billy. Yes. Billy made a good haul, didn't he?"

"You bet he did," affirmed Pokey. "Too bad you're goin' to leave us in a couple days. We got plenty of food now."

"I think," returned Delavan slowly, "that I was wrong about leaving. I'd better stay around."

"Say!" exclaimed the little man, "that's fine!" His watery blue eyes sparkled and he set his black hat at a jaunty angle. "Why, you'll be here for the trial, then."

"Yes, I'll be here for the trial. I hope the boy gets off." But Delavan was remembering the mark he had seen on the butt of the .45 and the significant gesture the Indian had made with his finger, and he smiled broadly down the empty street, pausing for a moment to greet a mythical horse wrangler much to the interest of Pokey Mackay.

CHAPTER THREE

N OW," exclaimed Pokey Mackay, rapping on the desk in the sheriff's office with the butt of his empty six-gun, "the court passes upon you, my son, the verdict of not guilty. We have every evidence that this crime, in all its monstrousness, was committed by another."

Delavan gave the front of the desk a stern look and shifted his weight in the chair beside the haughty Judge Mackay.

"But let me admonish you," continued Pokey in a deep voice, "that your entire life should be guided now by past experience. Let us see you no more with the men of crime, let us see you only with men of upstanding character and unquestionable honesty."

"That's right," echoed Delavan.

"And so, my son," said Pokey, "you may go home with your dear mother. That is all, madame." Pokey's eyes followed to the door and then, after sitting quite still for a space of a minute, sighed wearily.

"Sad case," Delavan remarked. "I'm glad it came out that way, aren't you, Judge?"

"Yes, I certainly am. Now, let's you and me go have a drink."

Together they entered the Palace Saloon where Delavan set out the drinks and had them charged to his own account.

As he sipped at his liquor, Pokey frowned suddenly as

though the place had suggested something to him. "I wonder where that feller Purcell is. I ain't seen him around here for . . . for . . . How long has it been, Ross?"

"Three months," informed Delavan over the rim of his glass.

"Funny thing. He used to show up around here every few weeks. Snooping around, you know. Wanted to get some tips from the way I handle this town." Pokey set his glass down with emphasis. "He ain't no good, that feller. Still, I was always pretty nice to him. When you're sheriff in a fine city like this, you got to be nice to feller peace officers, ain't you? I wonder why he don't come around."

"I don't think," replied Delavan, "that he'll be around for some little time."

"You mean on account of that sock I handed him? That hadn't ought to keep him away all that time."

Delavan whirled his glass thoughtfully and then poured out another drink. "No, I'm not thinking of that sock. What was his first name?"

"Give me one of those," said Pokey holding out his glass. "Them trials always make me awful thirsty someway. What was his first name, did you say? Edward. That was it. Edward Purcell."

"Edward Purcell," echoed Delavan with a thoughtful squint. "So I was right about it after all."

"Right about what?" demanded Pokey.

"Nothin'. Listen. Do any of your guns work?"

Pokey shifted his gaze out to the sunbaked street and moved a restless foot. "Now, to tell the truth, I can't say as they do. They would, of course, if they hadn't shipped me bum ammunition with that last freighter."

"Well," said Delavan in an even voice, "you'd better take this." He unbuckled his left-hand gun belt and gave it to Pokey.

"Say!" exclaimed Pokey. "That's fine! Look, it fits right square, don't it? I been wishin' you'd let me pack one of these six-guns for you. Looked as if you had all you could do to drag 'em around! I'm tickled to be able to give you a hand. And say! These denizens around here that like to rob things and shoot people had better watch out from now on!" Pokey climbed up on the bar and surveyed himself in the murky mirrors, turning from one side to the other to better see the figure he cut with the shiny weapon and belt.

Delavan tugged at the bottom of the frock coat. "Listen, Pokey. If it's all the same to you, we'd better get out along the street. We're going to have visitors. Bad ones."

Pokey's eyes blazed with excitement. "You mean that?"

"Yes, I saw the whole bunch about four miles away when we came in here. That's why I gave you the gun. They'll be a little more than a dust cloud now. Come on."

"Maybe," cried Pokey, "maybe it's Billy the Kid. That feller you was tellin' me about. Maybe he got wind of my billion-dollar gold mine."

"No," replied Delavan walking to the doorless doorway. "I've got a hunch this bunch would make Billy at his worst look like a Sunday school superintendent."

Pokey was excited before, but when he saw the cloud of

dust a mile to the east, his joy knew no bounds. "Do you really think," he pleaded, "that these fellers'll be outlaws?"

"I know it," Delavan affirmed. "Listen, Pokey. These gents won't know you're still here or anything about me. We'd better get along toward the hotel."

"The hotel!" howled Pokey. "You mean we ain't goin' to fight? You mean we ain't goin' to fire a shot?"

"Come along. There'll be plenty of shooting before this thing is over."

Pokey hitched at the .45 and followed Delavan into the New Yorker and up the stairs.

Kneeling out of sight below a windowsill on the second floor, Delavan checked over his gun and gave the Wells Fargo office a studious look. Pulling Pokey back from the window, Delavan shook his head. "No use gettin' anxious. They'll be along fast enough to suit you."

"You seem to know all about this," whispered Pokey. "Who are these fellers?"

Delavan laid his .45 on his knee and leaned against the wall. "You never heard of them. The leader's a gent named Ace Blanton and with him there'll probably be Mex Rojas and a couple other greasers."

"Sure, but what's that got to do with you?" asked Pokey, still whispering.

"Plenty!" Delavan looked out and then sat back against the wall. "But whatever you do, don't drill the only white man in the crowd. I want him alive."

"All right. I'll shoot him through the hip." Pokey spun the cylinder of the .45. "Why do you have to have him alive?"

"To keep myself from going to jail for murder. Now, listen. Don't shoot until they start to come out of the Wells Fargo office. When they do, just keep them away from their horses. Get it?"

"You bet I get it." Pokey listened to the approach of hoofbeats and then rubbed his sleeve over the rusty star on his black vest. "I'll show them varmints they can't come into a law-abidin' town and shoot it up!"

Ace Blanton, dwarfed, his face knife-edged and cruel, drew rein in the middle of Main Street and waited until his three men came abreast of his horse.

"I wonder where that old desert rat is," said Ace Blanton.

"Ah," coughed the huge Mex Rojas from under tangled strands of greasy black hair. "Eef he shows hees head, I weel . . ." He drew a significant finger across his throat.

With a laugh, Ace Blanton walked his horse to the hitchrack in front of the Wells Fargo office to dismount and secure his reins.

Delavan pushed aside the gun Pokey had started to aim. "Wait a while. We've got plenty of time."

With a fierce twist of his face, Pokey whispered, "Did you hear that ape call me a desert rat? I'll show him who's mayor of this town!"

The four, without any further parley, disappeared into the dimness of the office from whence came muffled footfalls and curses.

"Say!" exclaimed Pokey. "Those are the same fellers that romped in here before!"

"Sure. I knew it."

"How did you know it? You never saw them fellers." But Pokey's train of thought was completely blasted by the sudden explosion which made the buildings tremble. "My God! They're blowing the town up!"

"No," returned Delavan. "That was just the safe in there." With a bitter expression on his lean face, he watched the four scuttle back into the shack through the back door.

The ponies at the hitchrack were rearing excitedly and trying to break their reins, and Mex Rojas jumped out into the street to quiet them down.

"Rojas!" called Delavan. "Rojas!" The man stopped and gave the windows a mystified, horrified scrutiny. "Go back and tell Ace to throw his guns out into the street. I've got the lot of you covered!"

But Mex Rojas had other ideas and jerked his gun from its holster. Simultaneous with the action, a gun blazed beside Delavan's head and the man called Rojas slumped wearily forward, tried to catch himself, and then sprawled lifeless in the dust.

"How do you like that brand of shootin'?" shrilled Pokey. "Greasers are my special meat!"

From the doorway of the Wells Fargo office came a rasping thunder of words. "Delavan!" roared Ace Blanton. "I'll make buzzard meat out of you, you jackass!"

Delavan calmly looked through the sights of his Colt and sent a random shot into the dark interior across the street. "The next," he called out, "will rip you to bits. Throw down your hardware, Blanton. Your number's up!"

Delavan calmly looked through the sights of his Colt and sent a random shot into the dark interior across the street.

Wood shivered away from the panel above Delavan's head and a plume of smoke shot up from the doorway of the office.

"Say," cried Pokey, "I just had an idea!" Without waiting for Delavan's reaction, he went out of the room and ran down the stairs to make his way out through the back of the hotel.

With a puzzled frown at Pokey's disappearing back, Delavan turned and sent another shot into the doorway. At this rate, he reasoned, the fight would keep up all day and night would bring out a curtain behind which Ace could escape. Delavan had not counted on so much resistance.

A shot echoed from down the street to be followed, a moment later, from the upper section of town. Then, between shots, Delavan heard another directly below his window which was accompanied by a wild, Comanche war whoop. A guttural snarl preceded the next shot from the back of the Palace Saloon, and, almost before the echo had ceased, a report from the back of the blacksmith shop elicited a shrill yelp from the interior of the Wells Fargo office.

As he reloaded his smoking Colt, Delavan wondered where all the reinforcements had been gathered, for, while the shots only came one at a time, they seemed to be far too numerous in position to be accredited to one gun.

A greaser attempted to make a break through the back door of the office, presenting a fleeing back to Delavan for one brief instant. A curse was stayed on Delavan's lips by a crisp *Bang!* from the mow of the livery stable. The Mexican reeled back into sight, stumbling, tearing at his throat to fall in a crumpled pile.

A moment later, Pokey came into sight, running hard and low through the dust of the street. Bullets spurted about him and flame darted from an unseen window in the side of the Wells Fargo office. Try as he might, Delavan was unable to place a stop to the sniping, but he sighed with relief as he saw Pokey slide—as though he was making first base—into the cover of the sheriff's office. The sniping stopped and then firing was resumed through the doorway at the New Yorker Hotel.

Out of the corner of his eye, Delavan saw a loop whistle out of the sheriff's door to drop expertly over the neck of one of the horses at the hitchrack twenty feet away. The bronc reared and pawed air as the loop tightened about its neck. Flame leaped twice from the source of the rope and then, with the second shot, the reins of the animal parted and the lariat was tugged.

Keeping up a careful fire from the window, Delavan paused for a moment in surprise as he saw the roped bronc walk in through the door of the low building to completely disappear from sight.

Pokey's arm appeared again in the entrance of the building next to the Wells Fargo office, and it swung a wide loop. Unable to see more than a section of the arc made by the swinging rope, those in the small Wells Fargo building were powerless to do anything, for they did not suspect the next play until it was too late.

The loop jumped out and almost encircled the miniature false front of the outlaw's stronghold. Rapidly it came back to be cast again. This time it went neatly around the board front of the building.

Then, still covered by the sheriff's office, Pokey led the horse out to the side of the structure and looped the other end of the lariat about the horn.

Delavan smiled in sudden comprehension and redoubled his covering fire.

Pokey was shouting now in an ominous tone. "Hey, you! Ace Blanton and that other Mex! Can you hear me?"

Blanton's voice rasped out a reply. "If I could see you, you'd believe it, you little snipe!"

"Well, all I wanted to say is"—and here Pokey threw out his chest—"is that I'm about to pull that building down away from you. There are six gents over across the street just waiting for you rats to run out. Understand? I'll give you ten to come out. After that I quirt this here cow hoss and pull your office up by the roots. Get me?"

A long silence came from the Wells Fargo office and the grinning Delavan sat waiting and watching.

Pokey gave the rope an experimental tug and the false front groaned ominously.

"All right!" bawled Ace. "All right!" Two .45s described glinting arcs in the hot sunlight and threw up spurts of dust as they landed.

Their arms high in the air, Blanton and his greaser walked out, gazing fearfully, about to encounter the hungry tunnel of Pokey's Colt.

"C'mon, Delavan!" shouted Pokey. "Tell Billy and Jimmy

and Pete to keep those others under cover until we get the varmints penned up!"

"Hey, Billy!" shouted Delavan from the window. "Don't move until we come out of the sheriff's office!" Grinning, he withdrew his head and, in a minute, came out the front door of the New Yorker Hotel.

"Git in there!" ordered Pokey with a growl, and the silent pair walked into the sheriff's office where the clink of iron bars was soon heard.

Together, Pokey and Delavan came out and stood smiling at each other.

"I knew damned well," remarked Pokey, "that that building wouldn't have come down with a dozen ropes and hosses. But I had to take the chance. Come on, let's get a drink. This fightin' always makes me terrible thirsty."

CHAPTER FOUR

OVER breakfast the next morning, Pokey was very solemn. "Seems to me you're in a powerful hurry to get going."

"Well," said Delavan, "if you'd waited as long as I did to get that gent, you'd be in a hurry, too. Pokey, I been after Ace Blanton ever since they made me go broke down on the Panhandle. That was four years ago. Now do you blame me for wantin' to dust fast before he gets away from me?"

Pokey shook his head mournfully and then brightened. "Don't forget to tell Ed Purcell how I rounded up them varmints. It'll mortify him most to death."

"Edward Purcell," replied Delavan, "has been chewed up by the buzzards a long time ago. Three months to be exact."

"The hell you say!" exclaimed the surprised Pokey. "Who told you?"

"That was Purcell's gun that that Indian had in the store. It had the initials 'E. P.' on it."

"Well . . . well," stammered Pokey. "How did he get mixed up into this thing?"

"That's easy," said Delavan pushing back his plate. "Ace Blanton and Ed Purcell were in on that bank robbery. There weren't any witnesses and when Ace found out that I was on his trail he put the crime down to my name and sent Purcell up here. He sent Purcell to take me back and hang the crime on me. Now, if you'll come over to Jimmy's office for a minute, we'll see something else."

Too astounded to do more than sputter, Pokey followed Delavan across to the Wells Fargo office and stood goggling in the doorway.

The safe was shattered and, spilling out like green water, were thousands of dollars in crisp, new bills.

"That's the money that was taken from the bank," said Delavan.

"Well, how in hell did that stuff get there?" Pokey stepped to the blasted iron box and picked up a handful of bills.

"Remember the gents who came here the first time? Well, they were Blanton and his greasers. They cached that money in the safe, knowing that it would be poison until this thing blew over. And they knew they could blow up the safe any time they wanted to. So they came back and stuck in some dynamite and there you are."

"And this stuff was here for over three months and I didn't know it!" With dazed eyes, Pokey still looked at the bills.

"Purcell was sent up here by Ace Blanton for the money and for me. Purcell was supposed to hand the dough over to Blanton and then take me in dead. When he got out here and you socked him, he didn't know but what I was around with a gun and he didn't waste any time getting out. And then, Pokey, our friend Purcell went to meet Blanton and Blanton shot him, thinking the sheriff had cached the dough for himself." Delavan was picking up the bills and placing them in a neat pile on the roll-top desk. "There's a reward of two thousand dollars out for Blanton, dead or alive, and you get that. But

I've got to have that first thousand you found here on the floor
to make the wad complete."

"Sure," said Pokey, and he took the money out of the inner
pocket of his voluminous frock coat. "You mean that about
the reward?"

"Of course I do."

"Then I tell you what you do." Pokey sat down in the swivel
chair and folded his hands across his chest. "I've really got a
gold mine here. It ain't no billion-dollar mine but it'll pay.
I hear tell of a dry-washing process and a machine to do
it. Now, supposin' you buy one of those machines with the
reward money and then load up a couple pack mules with
molasses and such truck so we can live high and come back
here and help mine this place. Oh, yes. And you can import
a few Mexicans to do the digging and the work and to keep
up the town like it ought to be kept up. How do you like that
idea?"

Delavan smiled and leaned against the money he had
finished tying. "Like it? I'll say I like the idea. I haven't got
any place in the world anymore, so I might as well come out
here and help you run this place."

Later in the day, the departing cavalcade was formed in front
of the New Yorker Hotel and Pokey came up to glare at the
securely bound outlaws and shake Delavan by the hand.

Then Delavan brightened. "Say, Pokey, why don't you grab
that other hoss and come along? Do you good."

"No, sir," exclaimed Pokey. "My term of sheriff ain't expired
by a long ways and what do you think would happen to

this city if I went right off and left it? A mayor's got some responsibility!" Pokey stepped back and watched Delavan spur his horse and start out. "S'long. And don't stay away too long!"

"See you in a month!" shouted Delavan amid the yellow dust.

"There, Pete," said Pokey to the empty air, "goes a mighty fine young feller."

"Yes, sir, Mr. Mackay," returned Pokey. "I think the world and all of that gent."

STORY PREVIEW

NOW that you've just ventured through some of the captivating tales in the Stories from the Golden Age collection by L. Ron Hubbard, turn the page and enjoy a preview of *The Baron of Coyote River*. Join Lance Gordon, who's killed his father's slayers only to have a price put on his head, forcing him to join forces with a mystery man of the range. Even together, the pair stand little chance of bringing a gang of ruthless rustlers to account.

THE BARON OF
COYOTE RIVER

THE man who came from across Hell's Parade Ground was stumbling, weaving from side to side in the wagon tracks, dragging up a yellow curtain of lazy dust behind him.

His high-heeled boots were battered, his angoras were heavy with mud long since dry, his yellow hair was matted from an old wound.

But he still walked and he still had his saddle. The saddle alone told its story. Here was a rider without a mount, here was a puncher who had come far.

And those who watched him come from the shadowy 'dobe of Santos read his story long before he had arrived.

If this man came from nearby he would wear leather batwings, and he would have had better sense than to stab at Hell's Parade Ground afoot in August. And the men of Santos reasoned with narrow eyes that this man was an outlaw—and as such they would receive him.

Lance Gordon did not care what they thought of him. He was too spent and hot for that. The sizzling sun made him feel like a roast pig, lacking only an apple to be served at a buzzard's banquet.

He stumbled through the outskirts of the 'dobe settlement, swerved into the main stem and limped toward a place facetiously named the Diamond Palace Saloon. The twenty-nine-inch tapaderos trailed from the saddle behind him but the silver conchas were too smeared to shine.

He stopped for a moment in the sun and looked into the dim bar, then, taking a hitch in his already frazzled nerve, he made the last ten feet, to lean wearily against the mahogany.

The half-breed bartender left off polishing glasses. "Name your poison, stranger."

Lance Gordon paid no heed to the stray punchers who had gathered curiously at the door. With a heavy effort, he plumped the saddle down on the bar, giving it a push.

"How much will you give me for the rig?"

"I ain't buyin' rigs, stranger."

"It's Mex and it's worth plenty. Look here, I'll let you have it cheap enough."

"Sorry, stranger. But," he added with a calculating muddy eye on the saddle, "I might let you take it out in trade."

"You got a gun . . . and maybe some ammunition?"

"Well, a feller kicked off here last week and he kind of bequeathed me his gun as sort of payment on his bar bill."

"Make it the gun, plenty of bullets and a quart and it's a trade."

The bartender pulled the saddle toward him, noticing two bullet holes in the skirt. In its place he planted a belted Frontiersman Colt .45. He grudgingly added the bottle.

Lance Gordon heard a wondering murmur from the doorway and he glanced sideways without any great interest at the silhouettes of the punchers against the bright yellow sunlight outside. He picked up the gun and buckled it about him, pocketed the cartridges and took the whiskey bottle by the neck. Then, stumbling against tables, he made his way to the far corner of the room and sat down with his back firmly against the wall. That was another bad sign.

A tall man with a heavy black beard and colorless eyes came in and leaned up against the bar. He wore batwings of extreme design which bore down their length gaudy spades, hearts, clubs and diamonds. At the sides, lashed down tight and low, were two pearl-handled, gold-chased revolvers of late pattern. The hat was straight brimmed and stiff and he wore it rakishly. For all the expression and movement he made he might as well have been a rock butte jutting out of the desert.

"Come far, stranger?" said this one.

Lance Gordon frowned heavily and raised a drink to his lips, his hands shaking until the amber fluid slopped over his knuckles.

"You never can tell," said Lance.

Another murmur came from the doorway. Two men importantly shouldered their way through and took their stand in the center of the room. One was wearing a black vest and a dirty white shirt, the other wore a star glittering against a coat the color of dust.

"I'm sheriff here," said the man with the star. "Brant's the name."

"Not *the* Brant," said Lance with an unsteady smile.

Brant shoved his chest out a little. "That's me."

"Never heard of you," said Lance.

The tall bearded one smiled.

Brant scowled until his little pinched eyes were almost

invisible. His gray mustache bristled. "I came in here to find out what your business was in this town, stranger."

"That's easy," said Lance. "My business."

Brant took a step nearer, peering intently at the newcomer. He saw a disk of silver sparkle on Lance's chin thong and on closer inspection knew that the sparkle came from a set diamond there.

Brant began to smile and inch his fingers toward his gun. "I know you now. Your name's Lance Gordon, ain't it? I'd know that thong anyplace. You might as well come along peaceable-like. Don't seem they appreciated MacLeod's killing over in the Sierras."

Outside of an almost imperceptible tightening of his muscles, Lance received the news calmly. "Word travels fast, doesn't it?"

"About killers," said Brant, fingers closing over his revolver butt.

It did not seem to those who watched that Lance Gordon moved, but the gun he had just received from the bartender looked like a tunnel about to receive a train.

"I'm tired of running," said Lance. "I'm sick of it. It doesn't matter to you that MacLeod slaughtered a dozen men to get his land in the Nevadas. If you've got orders to send me back, then carry them out. But I'm not going—alive."

To find out more about *The Baron of Coyote River* and how you can obtain your copy, go to www.goldenagestories.com.

GLOSSARY

STORIES FROM THE GOLDEN AGE *reflect the words and expressions used in the 1930s and 1940s, adding unique flavor and authenticity to the tales. While a character's speech may often reflect regional origins, it also can convey attitudes common in the day. So that readers can better grasp such cultural and historical terms, uncommon words or expressions of the era, the following glossary has been provided.*

---

angoras: chaps (leather leggings the cowboy wears to protect his legs) made of goat hide with the hair left on.

appetite over tin cup: head over heels; bowled over.

batwings: long chaps (leather leggings the cowboy wears to protect his legs) with big flaps of leather. They usually fasten with rings and snaps.

Billy the Kid: (1859–1881) a nineteenth-century American frontier outlaw and gunman, reputed to have killed twenty-one men, one for each year of his life.

Bird Cage Opera: "Bird Cage Theater," also referred to as "The Bird Cage Opera House Saloon." This was a fancy way in the 1880s of describing a combination saloon, gambling hall and brothel.

brimstone: "fire-and-brimstone"; threatening punishment in the hereafter.

buckboard: buckboard wagon; a four-wheeled wagon of simple construction having a platform fastened directly to the axles with seating attached for the driver.

buffalo gun: .50-caliber Sharps rifle, also called the "Big Fifty," which weighed twelve pounds. Noted for its power and range, it was the almost unanimous choice among buffalo hunters. The drawbacks were the cost of ammunition and the fact that the rifle's accuracy was seriously affected by rapid fire (it had to be watered down constantly to keep from overheating).

bulldogging: throwing a calf or steer by seizing its horns and twisting its neck until the animal falls.

cat-eyed: said of a badman who has to be constantly watchful to keep from being "downed" by a rival. Most men of this type make it their business to sit with their backs to the wall, facing the door.

cayuse: used by the northern cowboy in referring to any horse. At first the term was used for the Western horse to set it apart from a horse brought overland from the East. Later the name was applied as a term of contempt to any scrubby, undersized horse. Named after the Cayuse Indian tribe.

century plant: a plant with grayish green leaves that takes ten to thirty years to mature and flowers just once before dying.

chinks: short leather chaps (leggings), usually fringed and stopping just below the knee, worn over the pants for protection.

chuck wagon: a mess wagon of the cow country. It is usually made by fitting, at the back end of an ordinary farm wagon, a large box that contains shelves and has a hinged lid fitted with legs that serves as a table when lowered. The chuck wagon is a cowboy's home on the range, where he keeps his bedroll and dry clothes, gets his food and has a warm fire.

Comanche: originally a part of the Shoshonean tribe, the Comanches emerged as a distinct group shortly before 1700. This coincided with their acquisition of the horse, which allowed them greater mobility in their search for better hunting grounds. Their original migration took them to southern plains extending from the Arkansas River to Central Texas. By the mid-1800s, they were supplying horses to French and American traders and settlers. Many of these horses were stolen and the Comanches earned a reputation as formidable horse and later cattle thieves.

cowpuncher: a hired hand who tends cattle and performs other duties on horseback; cowboy.

cow town: a town at the end of the trail from which cattle were shipped; later applied to towns in the cattle country that depended upon the cowman and his trade for their existence.

crik: creek.

cuspidor: a large bowl, often of metal, serving as a receptacle for spit, especially from chewing tobacco, in wide use during the nineteenth and early twentieth centuries.

Digger Indians: a name for Indians of the Southwest, Great Basin (between the Rockies and Sierra Nevada) or Pacific Coast. Most of these Indians were Shoshones or Paiutes. They were often called *Diggers* due to their practice of digging for roots.

drew rein: from "draw in the reins," meaning to slow down or stop by exerting pressure on the reins.

drill: shoot.

dry-washing: extracting gold from dry gravel by use of a machine.

dust: to depart.

false-fronted: a façade falsifying the size, finish or importance of a building.

faro: a gambling game played with cards and popular in the American West of the nineteenth century. In faro, the players bet on the order in which the cards will be turned over by the dealer. The cards were kept in a dealing box to keep track of the play.

fastnesses: remote and secluded places; secure places, well protected by natural features.

Fifty Girls Fifty: a chorus line of girls performing synchronized routines such as the can-can where they wear costumes with long skirts, petticoats and black stockings. The main features of the dance are the lifting up and manipulation of the skirts and high kicking.

fleeced: having deprived one of money or belongings by fraud, hoax or the like; swindled.

forked: mounted.

forked leather: mounted a saddled horse.

.45 or Colt .45: a single-action, .45-caliber, six-shot cylinder revolver first manufactured in 1873 by the Colt Firearms Company, a company founded by American firearms inventor Samuel Colt (1814–1862). The Colt, also known as the Peacemaker, was reliable, inexpensive and due to its popularity with cowboys became the symbol of the Old West.

forty-five or **.45:** a six-shot, single-action, .45-caliber revolver.

forty-one or **.41:** Derringer .41-caliber short pistol. Named for the US gunsmith Henry Deringer (1786–1868), who designed it.

furrin': foreign.

G-men: government men; agents of the Federal Bureau of Investigation.

GN: Great Northern Railway, the tracks of which extended more than 1,700 miles from Minnesota to Washington state.

gold-chased revolvers: gold-engraved metal, as ornamentation on a gun.

greensticked: the incomplete fracture of a bone in which one side is broken while the other is bent.

hammer-headed: stubborn, mean-spirited (of a horse).

hazed: drove (as cattle or horses) from horseback.

heeled: armed with a gun.

Henry: the first rifle to use a cartridge with a metallic casing rather than the undependable, self-contained powder, ball and primer of previous rifles. It was named after B. Tyler Henry, who designed the rifle and the cartridge.

hide-out: a gun, usually a short-barreled gun that can be hidden upon one's person.

hitchrack: a fixed horizontal rail to which a horse can be fastened to prevent it from straying.

Hood River: a county in Oregon, extending from Mt. Hood north to the Columbia River.

Hopi Indians: a Pueblo Indian people of northeast Arizona noted for their craftsmanship in basketry, pottery, silverwork and weaving.

hoss: horse.

ladino: a wild, unmanageable ranch animal.

lariat: a long noosed rope used for catching horses, cattle, etc.; lasso.

larrup: to strike; to thrash.

lath: made with narrow strips of wood formed into lattice.

lineback: having a stripe down its back that is of a different color from the rest of its body.

livery stable: a stable that accommodates and looks after horses for their owners.

longhorn: a name given the early cattle of Texas because of the enormous spread of their horns that served for attack and defense. They were not only mean, but the slightest provocation, especially with a bull, would turn them into an aggressive and dangerous enemy. They had lanky bodies and long legs built for speed. A century or so of running wild had made the longhorns tough and hardy enough to withstand blizzards, droughts, dust storms and attacks by other animals and Indians. It took a good horse with a good rider to outrun a longhorn.

mow: haymow; the upper floor of a barn or stable used for storing hay.

Nevadas: Sierra Nevada mountain range of eastern California, extending between the Sacramento and San Joaquin valleys and the Nevada border.

owl-hoot: outlaw.

papooses: Native American infants or very young children.

poke: a small sack or bag, usually a crude leather pouch, in which a miner carried his gold dust and nuggets.

pole-axing: striking down.

Pole Star: North Star; a star that is vertical, or nearly so, to the North Pole. Because it always indicates due north for an observer anywhere on Earth, it is important for navigation.

puncher: a hired hand who tends cattle and performs other duties on horseback.

quirt: 1. to lash or flog with a riding whip. 2. a riding whip with a short handle and a braided leather lash.

rag-tailed: "ragtag and bobtail"; describing a group of persons regarded as the lowest class.

redeye: cheap, strong whiskey.

rowels: the small spiked revolving wheels on the ends of spurs, which are attached to the heels of a rider's boots and used to nudge a horse into going faster.

run-over boots: old boots where the heel is so unevenly worn on the outside that the back of the boot starts to lean to one side and does not sit straight above the heel.

scatter-gun: a cowboy's name for a shotgun.

Scheherazade: the female narrator of *The Arabian Nights,* who during one thousand and one adventurous nights saved her life by entertaining her husband, the king, with stories.

Sharps: any of several models of firearms devised by Christian Sharps and produced by the Sharps Rifle Company until 1881. The most popular Sharps were "Old Reliable," the cavalry carbine, and the heavy-caliber, single-shot buffalo-hunting rifle. Because of its low muzzle velocity, this gun was said to "fire today, kill tomorrow."

Sierras: Sierra Nevada mountain range of eastern California extending between the Sacramento and San Joaquin valleys and the Nevada border.

single-action Army: Colt Single Action Army (SAA); a single-action, .45-caliber revolver holding six rounds. It was first manufactured in 1873 by the Colt Firearms Company, the armory founded by Samuel Colt (1814–1862). Initially produced for the Army to incorporate the latest metallic-cartridge technology, civilian versions were also made available in .32-, .38-, .41- and .44-calibers, among many others. The SAA, also referred to simply as Colt or the Peacemaker, gained popularity throughout the West and has become known as the "cowboy's gun."

single jacks: short-handled hammers with a three- to four-pound head. They are used to punch holes in rock.

sombrero: a Mexican style of hat that was common in the Southwest. It had a high-curved wide brim, a long, loose chin strap and the crown was dented at the top. Like cowboy hats generally, it kept off the sun and rain, fended off the branches and served as a handy bucket or cup.

spittoon: a container for spitting into.

Stetson: as the most popular broad-brimmed hat in the West, it became the generic name for *hat.* John B. Stetson was a master hat maker and founder of the company that has been making Stetsons since 1865. Not only can the Stetson stand up to a terrific amount of beating, the cowboy's hat has more different uses than any other garment he wears. It keeps the sun out of the eyes and off the neck; it serves as an umbrella; it makes a great fan, which sometimes is needed when building a fire or shunting cattle about; the brim serves as a cup to water oneself, or as a bucket to water the horse or put out the fire.

tapaderos: heavy leather around the front of stirrups to protect the rider's foot.

trail herd: a herd of cattle driven along a trail, especially from their home range to market.

truck: miscellaneous items.

varmints: those people who are obnoxious or make trouble.

wet stock: stolen cattle; cattle stolen from Mexico into Texas were taken across the Rio Grande River, and these were called "wet stock."

whang leather: tough leather adapted for strings, thongs, belt-lacing, etc., commonly made from calf hide.

whup into shape: "whip into shape"; to bring forcefully to a desired state or condition.

Winchester: an early family of repeating rifles; a single-barreled rifle containing multiple rounds of ammunition. Manufactured by the Winchester Repeating Arms Company, it was widely used in the US during the latter half of the nineteenth century. The 1873 model is often called "the gun that won the West" for its immense popularity at that time, as well as its use in fictional Westerns.

wrangler: a cowboy who takes care of the saddle horses.

yucca: any plant belonging or native to the warmer regions of the US, having pointed, usually rigid, sword-shaped leaves and clusters of white, waxy flowers.

L. Ron Hubbard
in the Golden Age
of Pulp Fiction

*In writing an adventure story
a writer has to know that he is adventuring
for a lot of people who cannot.
The writer has to take them here and there
about the globe and show them
excitement and love and realism.
As long as that writer is living the part of an
adventurer when he is hammering
the keys, he is succeeding with his story.*

*Adventuring is a state of mind.
If you adventure through life, you have a
good chance to be a success on paper.*

*Adventure doesn't mean globe-trotting,
exactly, and it doesn't mean great deeds.
Adventuring is like art.
You have to live it to make it real.*

—L. RON HUBBARD

L. Ron Hubbard
and American
Pulp Fiction

B ORN March 13, 1911, L. Ron Hubbard lived a life at
least as expansive as the stories with which he enthralled
a hundred million readers through a fifty-year career.

Originally hailing from Tilden, Nebraska, he spent his
formative years in a classically rugged Montana, replete with
the cowpunchers, lawmen and desperadoes who would later
people his Wild West adventures. And lest anyone imagine
those adventures were drawn from vicarious experience, he
was not only breaking broncs at a tender age, he was also
among the few whites ever admitted into Blackfoot society
as a bona fide blood brother. While if only to round out an
otherwise rough and tumble youth, his mother was that rarity
of her time—a thoroughly educated woman—who introduced
her son to the classics of Occidental literature even before
his seventh birthday.

But as any dedicated L. Ron Hubbard reader will attest, his
world extended far beyond Montana. In point of fact, and as the
son of a United States naval officer, by the age of eighteen he
had traveled over a quarter of a million miles. Included therein
were three Pacific crossings to a then still mysterious Asia, where
he ran with the likes of Her British Majesty's agent-in-place

L. Ron Hubbard, left, at Congressional Airport, Washington, DC, 1931, with members of George Washington University flying club.

for North China, and the last in the line of Royal Magicians from the court of Kublai Khan. For the record, L. Ron Hubbard was also among the first Westerners to gain admittance to forbidden Tibetan monasteries below Manchuria, and his photographs of China's Great Wall long graced American geography texts.

Upon his return to the United States and a hasty completion of his interrupted high school education, the young Ron Hubbard entered George Washington University. There, as fans of his aerial adventures may have heard, he earned his wings as a pioneering barnstormer at the dawn of American aviation. He also earned a place in free-flight record books for the longest sustained flight above Chicago. Moreover, as a roving reporter for *Sportsman Pilot* (featuring his first professionally penned articles), he further helped inspire a generation of pilots who would take America to world airpower.

Immediately beyond his sophomore year, Ron embarked on the first of his famed ethnological expeditions, initially to then untrammeled Caribbean shores (descriptions of which would later fill a whole series of West Indies mystery-thrillers). That the Puerto Rican interior would also figure into the future of Ron Hubbard stories was likewise no accident. For in addition to cultural studies of the island, a 1932–33

124

LRH expedition is rightly remembered as conducting the first complete mineralogical survey of a Puerto Rico under United States jurisdiction.

There was many another adventure along this vein: As a lifetime member of the famed Explorers Club, L. Ron Hubbard charted North Pacific waters with the first shipboard radio direction finder, and so pioneered a long-range navigation system universally employed until the late twentieth century. While not to put too fine an edge on it, he also held a rare Master Mariner's license to pilot any vessel, of any tonnage in any ocean.

Yet lest we stray too far afield, there is an LRH note at this juncture in his saga, and it reads in part:

"I started out writing for the pulps, writing the best I knew, writing for every mag on the stands, slanting as well as I could."

To which one might add: His earliest submissions date from the summer of 1934, and included tales drawn from true-to-life Asian adventures, with characters roughly modeled on British/American intelligence operatives he had known in Shanghai. His early Westerns were similarly peppered with details drawn from personal experience. Although therein lay a first hard lesson from the often cruel world of the pulps. His first Westerns were soundly rejected as lacking the authenticity of a Max Brand yarn

Capt. L. Ron Hubbard in Ketchikan, Alaska, 1940, on his Alaskan Radio Experimental Expedition, the first of three voyages conducted under the Explorers Club flag.

(a particularly frustrating comment given L. Ron Hubbard's Westerns came straight from his Montana homeland, while Max Brand was a mediocre New York poet named Frederick Schiller Faust, who turned out implausible six-shooter tales from the terrace of an Italian villa).

Nevertheless, and needless to say, L. Ron Hubbard persevered and soon earned a reputation as among the most publishable names in pulp fiction, with a ninety percent placement rate of first-draft manuscripts. He was also among the most prolific, averaging between seventy and a hundred thousand words a month. Hence the rumors that L. Ron Hubbard had redesigned a typewriter for faster keyboard action and pounded out manuscripts on a continuous roll of butcher paper to save the precious seconds it took to insert a single sheet of paper into manual typewriters of the day.

That all L. Ron Hubbard stories did not run beneath said byline is yet another aspect of pulp fiction lore. That is, as publishers periodically rejected manuscripts from top-drawer authors if only to avoid paying top dollar, L. Ron Hubbard and company just as frequently replied with submissions under various pseudonyms. In Ron's case, the

---

A MAN OF MANY NAMES

Between 1934 and 1950, L. Ron Hubbard authored more than fifteen million words of fiction in more than two hundred classic publications. To supply his fans and editors with stories across an array of genres and pulp titles, he adopted fifteen pseudonyms in addition to his already renowned L. Ron Hubbard byline.

Winchester Remington Colt
Lt. Jonathan Daly
Capt. Charles Gordon
Capt. L. Ron Hubbard
Bernard Hubbel
Michael Keith
Rene Lafayette
Legionnaire 148
Legionnaire 14830
Ken Martin
Scott Morgan
Lt. Scott Morgan
Kurt von Rachen
Barry Randolph
Capt. Humbert Reynolds

---

list included: Rene Lafayette, Captain Charles Gordon, Lt. Scott Morgan and the notorious Kurt von Rachen—supposedly on the lam for a murder rap, while hammering out two-fisted prose in Argentina. The point: While L. Ron Hubbard as Ken Martin spun stories of Southeast Asian intrigue, LRH as Barry Randolph authored tales of

L. Ron Hubbard, circa 1930, at the outset of a literary career that would finally span half a century.

romance on the Western range—which, stretching between a dozen genres is how he came to stand among the two hundred elite authors providing close to a million tales through the glory days of American Pulp Fiction.

In evidence of exactly that, by 1936 L. Ron Hubbard was literally leading pulp fiction's elite as president of New York's American Fiction Guild. Members included a veritable pulp hall of fame: Lester "Doc Savage" Dent, Walter "The Shadow" Gibson, and the legendary Dashiell Hammett—to cite but a few.

Also in evidence of just where L. Ron Hubbard stood within his first two years on the American pulp circuit: By the spring of 1937, he was ensconced in Hollywood, adopting a Caribbean thriller for Columbia Pictures, remembered today as *The Secret of Treasure Island*. Comprising fifteen thirty-minute episodes, the L. Ron Hubbard screenplay led to the most profitable matinée serial in Hollywood history. In accord with Hollywood culture, he was thereafter continually called upon

The 1937 Secret of Treasure Island, *a fifteen-episode serial adapted for the screen by L. Ron Hubbard from his novel,* Murder at Pirate Castle.

to rewrite/doctor scripts—most famously for long-time friend and fellow adventurer Clark Gable.

In the interim—and herein lies another distinctive chapter of the L. Ron Hubbard story—he continually worked to open Pulp Kingdom gates to up-and-coming authors. Or, for that matter, anyone who wished to write. It was a fairly unconventional stance, as markets were already thin and competition razor sharp. But the fact remains, it was an L. Ron Hubbard hallmark that he vehemently lobbied on behalf of young authors—regularly supplying instructional articles to trade journals, guest-lecturing to short story classes at George Washington University and Harvard, and even founding his own creative writing competition. It was established in 1940, dubbed the Golden Pen, and guaranteed winners both New York representation and publication in *Argosy*.

But it was John W. Campbell Jr.'s *Astounding Science Fiction* that finally proved the most memorable LRH vehicle. While every fan of L. Ron Hubbard's galactic epics undoubtedly knows the story, it nonetheless bears repeating: By late 1938, the pulp publishing magnate of Street & Smith was determined to revamp *Astounding Science Fiction* for broader readership. In particular, senior editorial director F. Orlin Tremaine called for stories with a stronger *human element*. When acting editor John W. Campbell balked, preferring his spaceship-driven tales, Tremaine enlisted Hubbard. Hubbard, in turn, replied with the genre's first truly *character-driven* works, wherein heroes are pitted not against bug-eyed monsters but the mystery and majesty of deep space itself—and thus was launched the Golden Age of Science Fiction.

The names alone are enough to quicken the pulse of any science fiction aficionado, including LRH friend and protégé, Robert Heinlein, Isaac Asimov, A. E. van Vogt and Ray Bradbury. Moreover, when coupled with LRH stories of fantasy, we further come to what's rightly been described as the foundation of every modern tale of horror: L. Ron Hubbard's immortal *Fear*. It was rightly proclaimed by Stephen King as one of the very few works to genuinely warrant that overworked term "classic"—as in: *"This is a classic tale of creeping, surreal menace and horror. . . . This is one of the really, really good ones."*

L. Ron Hubbard, 1948, among fellow science fiction luminaries at the World Science Fiction Convention in Toronto.

To accommodate the greater body of L. Ron Hubbard fantasies, Street & Smith inaugurated *Unknown*—a classic pulp if there ever was one, and wherein readers were soon thrilling to the likes of *Typewriter in the Sky* and *Slaves of Sleep* of which Frederik Pohl would declare: *"There are bits and pieces from Ron's work that became part of the language in ways that very few other writers managed."*

And, indeed, at J. W. Campbell Jr.'s insistence, Ron was regularly drawing on themes from the Arabian Nights and

129

so introducing readers to a world of genies, jinn, Aladdin and Sinbad—all of which, of course, continue to float through cultural mythology to this day.

At least as influential in terms of post-apocalypse stories was L. Ron Hubbard's 1940 *Final Blackout*. Generally acclaimed as the finest anti-war novel of the decade and among the ten best works of the genre ever authored—here, too, was a tale that would live on in ways few other writers imagined.

Portland, Oregon, 1943; L. Ron Hubbard, captain of the US Navy subchaser PC 815.

Hence, the later Robert Heinlein verdict: "Final Blackout *is as perfect a piece of science fiction as has ever been written.*"

Like many another who both lived and wrote American pulp adventure, the war proved a tragic end to Ron's sojourn in the pulps. He served with distinction in four theaters and was highly decorated for commanding corvettes in the North Pacific. He was also grievously wounded in combat, lost many a close friend and colleague and thus resolved to say farewell to pulp fiction and devote himself to what it had supported these many years—namely, his serious research.

But in no way was the LRH literary saga at an end, for as he wrote some thirty years later, in 1980:

"Recently there came a period when I had little to do. This was novel in a life so crammed with busy years, and I decided to amuse myself by writing a novel that was pure *science fiction."*

That work was *Battlefield Earth: A Saga of the Year 3000*. It was an immediate *New York Times* bestseller and, in fact, the first international science fiction blockbuster in decades. It was not, however, L. Ron Hubbard's magnum opus, as that distinction is generally reserved for his next and final work: The 1.2 million word *Mission Earth*.

> **Final Blackout**
> *is as perfect a piece of science fiction as has ever been written.*
>
> —Robert Heinlein

How he managed those 1.2 million words in just over twelve months is yet another piece of the L. Ron Hubbard legend. But the fact remains, he did indeed author a ten-volume *dekalogy* that lives in publishing history for the fact that each and every volume of the series was also a *New York Times* bestseller.

Moreover, as subsequent generations discovered L. Ron Hubbard through republished works and novelizations of his screenplays, the mere fact of his name on a cover signaled an international bestseller. . . . Until, to date, sales of his works exceed hundreds of millions, and he otherwise remains among the most enduring and widely read authors in literary history. Although as a final word on the tales of L. Ron Hubbard, perhaps it's enough to simply reiterate what editors told readers in the glory days of American Pulp Fiction:

He writes the way he does, brothers, because he's been there, seen it and done it!

THE STORIES FROM THE GOLDEN AGE

Your ticket to adventure starts here with the Stories from the Golden Age collection by master storyteller L. Ron Hubbard. These gripping tales are set in a kaleidoscope of exotic locales and brim with fascinating characters, including some of the most vile villains, dangerous dames and brazen heroes you'll ever get to meet.

The entire collection of over one hundred and fifty stories is being released in a series of eighty books and audiobooks. For an up-to-date listing of available titles, go to www.goldenagestories.com.

AIR ADVENTURE

FAR-FLUNG ADVENTURE

SEA ADVENTURE

134

TALES FROM THE ORIENT

The Devil—With Wings　　*Pearl Pirate*
The Falcon Killer　　*The Red Dragon*
Five Mex for a Million　　*Spy Killer*
Golden Hell　　*Tah*
The Green God　　*The Trail of the Red Diamonds*
Hurricane's Roar　　*Wind-Gone-Mad*
Inky Odds　　*Yellow Loot*
Orders Is Orders

MYSTERY

The Blow Torch Murder　　*The Grease Spot*
Brass Keys to Murder　　*Killer Ape*
Calling Squad Cars!　　*Killer's Law*
The Carnival of Death　　*The Mad Dog Murder*
The Chee-Chalker　　*Mouthpiece*
Dead Men Kill　　*Murder Afloat*
The Death Flyer　　*The Slickers*
Flame City　　*They Killed Him Dead*

FANTASY

SCIENCE FICTION

WESTERN

Aim for Adventure in Coyote River!

Lance Gordon killed his father's murderer in a fair fight, but now he's got a price on his head and has been running from the law ever since.

Cornered by men of the US Cavalry in Santos, Lance gets rescued by a mystery man who convinces him to join forces and go after a notorious cattle rustler up the infamous Coyote River.

Even together the pair stands barely a chance of bringing the gang of thieves to account, much less dealing with the soldiers still hot on their trail.

Get
The Baron of Coyote River

JOIN THE PULP REVIVAL
America in the 1930s and 40s

Pulp fiction was in its heyday and 30 million readers were regularly riveted by the larger-than-life tales of master storyteller L. Ron Hubbard. For this was pulp fiction's golden age, when the writing was raw and every page packed a walloping punch.

That magic can now be yours. An evocative world of nefarious villains, exotic intrigues, courageous heroes and heroines—a world that today's cinema has barely tapped for tales of adventure and swashbucklers.

Enroll today in the Stories from the Golden Age Club and begin receiving your monthly feature edition selected from more than 150 stories in the collection.

You may choose to enjoy them as either a paperback or audiobook for the special membership price of $9.95 each month along with FREE shipping and handling.

CALL TOLL-FREE: 1-877-8GALAXY
(1-877-842-5299) OR GO ONLINE TO
www.goldenagestories.com
AND BECOME PART OF THE PULP REVIVAL!